Morganwg Iolo

Poems, lyric and pastoral

Vol. I

Morganwg Iolo

Poems, lyric and pastoral
Vol. I

ISBN/EAN: 9783744715270

Printed in Europe, USA, Canada, Australia, Japan

Cover: Foto ©Andreas Hilbeck / pixelio.de

More available books at **www.hansebooks.com**

POEMS,

LYRIC and PASTORAL.

VOL. I.

[Price Ten Shillings.]

POEMS,

LYRIC AND PASTORAL.

IN TWO VOLUMES.

By *EDWARD WILLIAMS*,
Bardd wrth Fraint a Defod Beirdd Ynys Prydain.

VOL. I.

Noddais i 'mrŷd yn addwyn
Er yn fâb yr Awen fwyn,
Yn iâs ir ei naws eirian
Fy mŷd i gyd oedd y Gân ;
I'mhoen fyth ! am bŷan o fai
Un o'm Ceraint ni m carai.

IOLO MORGANWG.

Quod ſi me Lyricis vatibus inſeres
Sublimi feriam ſydera vertice.

HOR.

LONDON:

Printed, for the AUTHOR, by J. NICHOLS ;
And ſold by J. JOHNSON, Nᵒ 72, St. Paul's Church-
Yard; J. OWEN, Nᵒ 168, Piccadilly; E. WILLIAMS,
Nᵒ 11, Strand; DARTON and HARVEY, Grace-
church Street; by all the Bookſellers in Bath ;
FLETCHER, Oxford; MERRILL, Cambridge;
BROWN, and LLOYD, Briſtol ; HARWARD,
Cheltenham ; and PRITCHARD,
Philadelphia.

1794.

THESE VOLUMES ARE,

BY PERMISSION,

AND WITH

THE RESPECT OF GRATITUDE,

DEDICATED TO

HIS ROYAL HIGHNESS

GEORGE PRINCE OF WALES,

BY HIS MOST HUMBLE SERVANT,

EDWARD WILLIAMS.

CONTENTS.

The POEMS are in Roman Characters; the NOTES in Italic.

A 4

14. The

3

27. Damon's

Page

A 5

THESE

PREFACE.

MY little publication appears after a pretty long delay. Some obftacles occurred from the nature of my fituation in life: thefe were unavoidable, but moftly unforefeen ; others were thrown in my way by the mean machinations of Envy, that appears to have been hurt at the fuccefs and valuable friendfhip s that, for a little while, I met with at the opening of my fubfcription.

I had unfortunately, or rather foolifhly, repofed confidence in fome that I once thought my friends ; they became thus poffeffed of the knowledge how and where to injure me—and they did it—let them enjoy it.

I had, and ftill have, an intention of going to America, partly to fly from the numerous injuries I have received from the boafted laws of this land, that are not, whatever one REEVES, or his brother *Bear-monger*, of Holborn-Hill, may fay, made equally for the poor as for the rich ; and hardly an inftance can be produced, where a poor man, unbacked by wealthy friends, ever obtained juftice in our Law-Courts. Another motive is to a certain the truth of an opinion, prevalent in *Wales*, on good authority,

that

that there are ftill exifting, in the interior parts of the
American Continent, the remains of a *Welfh Colony*
that went over there in the twelfth Century under
the conduct of *Madoc*, the fon of *Owen Gwynedd*,
Prince of Wales. Some frivolous anecdote-hunter
inferted an account of my intention in one of the
Bath Papers, whence it was copied, in moft of the
London and many of the Country papers, with an
attention that furprized me, on fo trifling a fubject.
My enemies made a very good handle of this for the
dagger that was now drawn againft me : a report
was, whifperingly, circulated, that my Poems were
not at the prefs ; that I was going (fome faid I was
gone) to America, with my fubfcribers' money in
my pocket. It was long before I heard any thing of
this rumour, which acquired fome colour from my
work not appearing at the time that I had rafhly pro-
mifed it ; for, I was as ignorant of the nature of my
undert_king, and of the printing bufinefs, as any
one can well be. I was dilatory from other caufes
alfo : I was far from home and my family, where all
my little portion of happinefs was centered : I was
alfo confcious of the numerous defects and crudities
of my pieces, which made me frequently linger over
them befo·e I would put them to the prefs, whilft a
dejection thus occafioned difqualified me for making
fome amendments that I faw fo very requifite. There
were gentlemen of the firft abilities that would have
affifted me ; but I could not think of accepting their
very

very kind offers; for, I was from the beginning determined not to put the least imposition on the public, but to give them the real unsophisticated productions of the *self-tutored Journeyman Mason:* under such a mental depression, I am convinced, that I have sometimes rather injured than improved my pieces. Some may not admit these things as an apology; but they were occasioned by sensibilities that I am not ashamed of: and *all* will not blame me.

About November 1792, I had printed my Poems as far as half the second volume, my little stock of cash failed, and I had not the courage to mention this to my printer; who, from what I have since experienced, would have been my friend, on this occasion. I informed my friends (why do I call them so?) of this: they had, *unsolicited*, promised assistance to me, if necessary, had even *urged* me to apply for it without any scruple; but all was silence; subscriptions that, in some places, had been collected for me were with-held. I did not yet see the cause. I wrote an account of these things to Mrs. and Miss HARRIET BOWDLER, of Bath; and these most amiably benevolent Ladies, to whom I had before been under a thousand obligations of the first magnitude, supplied · me with what I wanted as soon as the post could bring it. I am on similar occasions under the same obligations to my excellent friends in London, Mr. OWEN JONES and Mr. WILLIAM OWEN. These Ladies and Gentlemen will dispense with those common-place phrases that express *hypocrisy* rather than gratitude.

Every

Every thing would have been very well now, and my Poems would foon have appeared; but for, what I had always dreaded, an account of the death of one of my *dear children, a favourite little girl*, with whom went more by far of the joys of my life than can ever be recovered in this world.—I went home immediately, and there, for eight or nine months, I remained. I forgive every thing to my enemies but their having been the means of detaining me from home when my *pretty little infant* was in the hour of death calling upon me. There are a few, and they are of the moſt valuable part of mankind, to whom this circumſtance will be no bad apology for the additional year of delay: I would not have been thus querulous, but that an apology was due to my fubfcribers; and what could it be but the truth ?

To thofe numerous Ladies and Gentlemen, by whom I have been thus *patronized*, I am, and ſhall be through life, gratefully thankful; and I truſt that none will be offended at me for printing the names of my moſt diſtinguiſhed friends in *Italics*, with now and then an &c. Their number was too great to be otherwife thanked in this place.

Some of my beſt friends have urged me to give fome anecdotes of my life. I have little of any thing to fay worth notice on this occafion. I was fo very unhealthy whilſt a child (and I have continued fo), that it was thought uſeleſs to put me to fchool,.

where

where my three brothers were kept for many years. I learned the alphabet before I can well remember, by feeing my father infcribe grave-ftones. My mother, whofe maiden name was MATTHEWS, was the daughter of a gentleman who had wafted a pretty fortune : fhe had been well educated; fhe taught me to read in a volume of *Songs*, intituled *The Vocal Mifcellany*; for, I could not be prevailed upon to be taught from any other book. My mother-fang agreeably, and I underftood that fhe learned her fongs from this book, which made me fo very defirous of learning it. This I did in a fhort time, and hence, I doubt not, my original turn for poetry. There is no truth in that old adage, *Poeta nafcitur, non fit*; for, I will venture to fay, that a Poetical and every other Genius is *made* by fome accident in early life, making an indelible impreffion on the tender mind of infancy.

I could buy no books : there was not at this time a fingle bookfeller, except itinerant-, that fold Welfh books, in all *Wales*. The whole of my (or rather my mother's) little library confifted of the *Bible*, fome of *Pope's* works. *Lintott's Mifcellany*, *Steele's Mifcellany*, *Randolph's Poems*, *Milton's Poetical Works*, a few volumes of the *Spectator*, *Tatler*, and *Guardian*, *The Whole Duty of Man*, *Browne's Religio Medici*, and *Golding's Tranflation of Ovid's Metamorphofes*, in the black letter, which I foon was able to read; and, with thefe, two or three books of arithmetic which

. my

my mother procured for me; and it was ſhe that taught me to *gvrite*, and the firſt five or ſix rules of *arithmetic*, with ſomething of *muſic*.

My firſt attempts in Poetry were in Welſh, that being the country *vernaculum*, though Engliſh was the language of my father's houſe. In 1770, my beſt of mothers died; I was then, though twenty-three years of age, as ignorant of the world almoſt - as a new-born child; this I gradually found by wo-ful experience. I had worked at my father's trade ſince I was nine years of age; but I never, from a child, aſſociated with thoſe of my age, never learned their diverſions. I returned every night to my mo-ther's fire-ſide, where I talked or read with her; if ever I walked out, it was by myſelf in unfrequented places, woods, the ſea-ſhore, &c. for I was very penſive, melancholy, and very *ſtupid*, as all but my mother thought; when a chearful fit occurred, it was wild extravagance generally.

After my mother's death I could no longer be happy at home, where ſhe was *never more to be ſeen.* I rambled for ſome years over a great part of Eng-land and Wales; my ſtudies were, during this time, chiefly *Architecture*, and the *other ſciences* that my trade required. In 1773, I went into *Kent*, where I ſtayed for near four years. I had been two or three years in *London, Briſtol*, &c. a return to rural objects had a pleaſing and powerful effect on my mind; this, and meeting with Dr. AIKIN's *Eſſays on Song-writing*,

which

which gave me much pleafure, revived my poetical
tafte, and I wrote many of the pieces contained in
thefe volumes in *Kent.* In 1777, I returned to
London, and foon after into *Wales* ; and a reftora-
tion to the fcenes of youth preferved and heightened
my paffion for poetry. In 1781, I married, and gradually, as my family increafed, was obliged to decline my hitherto pleafing ftudy. In 1790, the general election fupplied me with an occafion to fcrib-
ble fome trifles which introduced my verfes into
fome notice, and I was encouraged to print them by
fubfcription. I thus became fupplied with every
would-be literary *fool's* apology for expofing myfelf
to public ridicule; the *Advice of Friends.* This I ima-
gine is more than enough of my hiftory ; it is of no
importance to any one to know how many ftones I
hewed, or on how many grave-ftones I have infcribed
vile doggrel. Anecdotes of original impreffions on
the human mind may be of fome philofophical ufe ;
and I have here honeftly given my own. Unavoidable egotifms will be pardoned.

I repeat once more, that there is not in thefe volumes a fingle line or epithet that is not my own:
whenever a fault has been pointed out, or an im-
provement fuggefted, the removal of one, and the
accomplifhment of the other, was always my own attempt ; for, as I before obferved, I would not impofe
on the public on one hand, and I would exercife my
own faculties on the other. Corrections and improve-
ments

ments by fuperior learning and abilities are faid to
have taken place in fome productions of felf-cultiva-
ted Genius that have appeared; this is very repre-
henfible ; Philofophers read thefe things, and they
fhould not be deceived, for the fake of inveftigating
the properties and powers of the human mind under
all circumftances, advantages, and difadvantages, rather than for any intrinfic merit that thefe our crude
fcribblings poffefs.

Some of my beft pieces are ftill unprinted, as I
could not in time recover copies from thofe to whom
I had lent them, not having kept duplicates. I am
forry for this, but I cannot help it ; my beft pieces
were certainly due to my fubfcribers ; but to delay
the work longer could not be done with any propriety.

The Etymology of Britain, in one of my notes, is my
own ; and, I will venture to fay, the true one : indeed, this has been very freely acknowleged by the
beft *Welfh Critics*; yet, very ftrange ! it has never before appeared, unlefs lately from my communications.
I have in feveral places aimed at rectifying fome
miftakes of modern *Welfh Hiftorians*, gentlemen (if
they may be fo called) of *no confcience*, who are partial
to every thing but *Truth*. The true hiftory of the
Ancient Welfh Bards is wilfully fuppreffed in favour
of the wildeft preconcep/ions and abfurdeft theories
that could ever enter the brain of the moft barbarous
Goth.

I have

I have fome *general*, but no *perfonal*, fatire ; there is too much *Priefcraft* amongft every fect; too much *Kingcraft* in all, even *Republican*, Governments ; yet there are many *good Priefs* ; and, I believe, a brace of *good Kings* may be found; at leaft I will venture on *One ⁕*.

I have always, with an *Ancient Briton's warm pride*, preferved the freedom of my thoughts, and the independence of my mind : thefe fhall not be fubjected to any thing but my own confcience. Wherever I meet with *fcoundrelifm*, though captained by ever fo GREAT A NAME, my pen fhall have all the liberty of my fentiments ; I poffefs a trade, and, in that, *independence*. I doubt not but that numberlefs errors of judgement may be found in fome things that I have written. Other things may be deemed *imprudent* ; but *prudence* and *confcience* never walk hand in hand.

The merit that my Poems poffefs is very little indeed, but I hope that they have no taint of that immorality that fweeps, a powerful deluge, over the world ; I have declared myfelf the friend of *Peace*, *Benevolence*, *Liberty*, and the tranfcendently lovely *Chriftian Religion*. Why is it prefumptuous in me to hope that my fentiments may diffufe for a little while a feeble glimmer of glow-worm light over a very fmall part of the world ? Who knows but that in the bright conftellation of ftars of the firft magnitude,

---

⁕ Our Welfh Bard probably means the KING OF KINGS.
Printer's Devil.

that

that now illumine the Horizon of Truth, I may be
one of the feeblest; at least I would not for the
world be a *cloud* in it: to these sentiments I have sa-
crificed more than can yet be made known of that
vile infernal stuff called *Prudence*, that, though mis-
nomered a virtue, is always infallibly characteristic of
a *knave* or a *slave.*

The account of the *Bardic Triades* was drawn up
in great haste, and under anxieties that admitted of
no cool attention: this was, at the desire of some
friends, substituted in the room of the poems that
were intended originally: I too late observe it full of
inaccuracies and *blockheadisms.* The originals of these
Triades are in the *Silurian* (which is the *most ancient*)
dialect and orthography. I mention this to obviate
the carpings of those who, properly speaking, know
no dialect. The *Silurian* differs in many particulars
from the *Biblical* dialect of modern writers. To
attempt an investigation of the true sense of the very
obscure term *Abred* would have required a longer
dissertation than I had room for; and, probably, my
abilities would have failed me.

I have in one passage mentioned a *qualified sense* in
which the *Christian Bards and Druids* believed the
Metempsychosis: this was, that the depraved soul of
man passes in a state beyond the grave into progres-
sive modes of existence corresponding with the na-
tures of Earthly worms and brutes, into whom, in
the literal sense, the Aboriginal or Patriarchal Druids
believed

believed it paſſed. TALIESIN places this proba-
tionary, diveſtigating, or purifying, *Metempſychoſis* in
the *Hell* of *Chriſtianity*, whence the ſoul gradually
riſes again to *Felicity*, the way for it having been
opened by *Jeſus Chriſt*; for, this is his obvious meau-
ing, where he ſays,

> *Nifer a fuant yn anghyffred*
> Uffern *oer gwaredred*
> *Hyd bumoes Byd,*
> *Hyd pan ddillyngwys* Criſt *gaethiwed*
> *O ddyfnfais affwys* Abred,
> *Maint dyddwg* Duw *trwy nodded.*

i.e. multitudes were, ignorant of their ſtate, in Hell,
in the miſerable progreſſion of deliverance, during
the world's five ages ; until releaſed by *Chriſt* from
the captivities of the immenſe deep, of the abyſs of
Abred; all thoſe has GOD taken into his protection.

. I have probably miſtaken the ſenſe of ſome obſcure
paſſages. I wiſh ſome ingenious Welſh critic, and
there are many ſuch, would handle theſe curious
matters ; they are of great importance in Britiſh
Hiſtory, and throw new and great lights on it.

I have ſome thoughts of tranſlating all the *Bardic
Triades :* ſhould ſuch an intention be encouraged by
the public opinion of the ſhort extracts here given,
I will in the courſe of the enſuing ſummer, *with per-
miſſion of Providence*, give my tranſlation with the
originals to the preſs.

I wiſh that it had been in my power to diſcharge
more fully my very great obligations to a generous
public,

public, to my subscribers in particular, my real patrons: perhaps, but I care not, I may be a little tautological in attempting to express my gratitude: I have nothing to render but these feeble attempts.

External appearances are such, that many are supposed to be my friends who have been in reality very much my foes; but the world must remain undeceived: I am not inclined to publish *truths* that will involve me in a torrent of misrepresentation, obloquy, and abuse; there are many that "*will never pardon me for the injuries they have done me.*" Such is my case: and where is that man who, being a little advanced in life, has not experienced much of what is very similar; more than will be prudent for him, if he loves peace, ever to publish? Could I with propriety boast of any part of my conduct in life, it should be that in particular which has excited the Envy, and, of course, Enmity of some who will better than the public at large understand what I here allude to.

If any sentiment or trait in my very humble productions should procure me some friendship, or some favourable opinion of me from the Public, I freely confess that my happiness will be very much increased. If any thing of this nature comes from the *Good*, I shall care nothing for what of a different kind I may experience from what in the *vulgar accep-tation* we call the *Great*.

London, Jan. 1, 1794.

Translations

Translations of the Welsh Motto in the Title Page:

1. Whilft yet a child I lov'd the Mufe,
   Fix'd on her charms were all my views ;
   When came her thrilling thoughts along,
   My worlds all center'd in her fong.
   Hence what unpardon'd faults arofe,
   Converting *friends* to bitter *foes*.

   ———

2. Warm from a child I lov'd the Bardic Mufe,
   My worlds of blifs all center'd in her views ;
   Sweet Fancy revell'd in my thrilling heart :
   But this warm paffion for the tuneful art
   Was deem'd a crime, was mark'd with bitter
      blame,
   Till ev'ry *friend* a ruthlefs *foe* became.

   ———

3. From infant years I lov'd the Mufe,
      And woo'd her to my feeble arms ;
   Defpifing Wealth, I fix'd my views
      On fmiling Fancy's floral charms ;
   But *Envy's* hate purfues my rhime,
      Though breathing peace the ditty flows ;
   The Bardic fong is deem'd a crime,
      And former *friends* are now my *foes*.

   ———

IOLO MORGANWG, the Author's *Bardic name* con-
formable to ancient ufage.

In Englifh, EDWARD of GLAMORGAN.

E R.

[xxiv]

E R R A T A.
V O L. I.
Page Line
15   3 *for* ranking r. rankling.
122 13   gellid r. gelid.
104 6   ANON. r. SAVAGE.
195 20   CASSIVELLANNUS r. CASSIVELLAU-
       NUS.
203 7   doves r. does (i. e. female deer).
209 4   London r. London, &c.

CORRIGENDA.
44 10 r. thus:
Here peacefully glide my foft moments along.
71 3 r. And Heav'n's eternal bloom, &c.

V O L. II.
126 7 r. thus:
Through dangers—wild rivers and rocks.
128 14   *gorfod* r. *gorfod.*
ibid. 22   *anfoes* r. *anfoes.*
132 5 *for* thl r. till.
138 11   afcending fkies r. afcending the fkies.
227 17   PLENNYNDD r. PLENNYDD.
229 22   *ofer-* r. *ofer-.*
235 13   *Gwanhanfod* r. *Gwahanfod.*
237 ult.   *fes* r. *fif.*
248 6   add r and.
251 21   *mwyaf bo* r. *bo mwyaf.*

SUBSCRIBERS NAMES.

His Royal Highness
GEORGE PRINCE OF WALES.

A

Earl of ABERGAVENNY, 6 sets
Mr. Ady
John Aikin, M. D. &c.
George Edw. Allen, Esq.
Miss Aldsworth
Rev. Christ. Anstey, A. M.
Christopher Anstey, Esq. &c.
Mrs. Anstey
Arthur Anstey, Esq.
Captain Anstey
Miss Anstey
Sir William André
Mr. André
Miss André
Miss Louisa André
Arthur Annesley, Esq.
LADY ARCHER
Mr. Arding, Merton College, Oxon
Mr. Thomas Arrow
Samuel Athaws, Esq.

Mr. M. Atkinson
Sir John Aubrey, Bart.
Lady Aubrey
Richard Aubrey, Esq. 6 sets, &c.
Miss Aubrey

B

Mr. Bacon, Statuary
Edward Bates, Esq.
Miss Bateman
Winthrop Baldwin, Esq.
Mrs. Ball, 2 sets, &c.
Thomas Bathurst, Esq.
Rev. James Bannister
John Bassett, Esq.
Rev. Thomas Bassett, &c.
Copleston Warr Bampfylde, Esq.
Mr. Baker, Baliol College, Oxford

VOL. I.

b

Rev.

Rev. *Mr. Baxter*, A. M.
Fellow of Jesus College,
Oxford
Mrs. Barbauld
Mrs. Barrett, &c.
Mrs. E. Barrett, &c.
Mr. J. Barratt, Bookseller, Bath, &c.
DUKE of BEAUFORT
DUCHESS of BEAUFORT
LADY BEAUMONT
Richard Bevan, Esq.
Mrs. Bevan
John Bennet, Esq.
Mrs. Belli
Rev. Mr. Bere
Mrs. Beach
Miss Benson
Rev. *Thomas Belsham*, Tutor in Divinity at Hackney College
Rev. *Mr. Blomberg*
Mrs. Bifs, &c.
Samuel Boddington, Esq.
Mrs. Bowdler, 12 sets, &c.
Miss Bowdler
Miss Harriet Bowdler, 12 sets &c.
John Bowdler, Esq. &c.
Thomas Bowdler, Esq. &c.
Rev. *W. L. Bowles*, 4 sets, &c.
WILLIAM BOWLES, *Generalissimo of the Creek Nation*
Mr. W. Bowen
Mrs. Bowen
Rev. John Bowen

Mr. Bootle, Christ Church College, Oxford
John Bordieu, Esq.
James Boswell, Esq.
Hon. Mrs. *Boscawen*
H. *Bosanquet*, Esq. &c.
Mr. Brakespeare
Citoyen I. P. BRISSOT
Thomas Bridges, Esq.
Owen Tudor Brigstocke, A. B. Fellow of Jesus College, Oxford
Mr. Brown, Bookseller, Bristol
Miss Bruce, &c.
Dr. Burgh, York
Rev. Dr. Buckner, Archdeacon of Chichester
Mrs. M. Buckle
Mr. Bushby, Pembroke College, Oxford
Charles Burney, Mus. D. &c.
Miss Burney, &c.
EARL of BUTE, 6 sets
John Butler, Esq.
Miss Byet

C

Mr. Cannings, Christ-Church College, Oxford
Rev. Thos. Cantley, Trinity College, Cambr.
Sir *John Caldwell*, Bart. 3 sets, &c.
Lady Caldwell

I

John

John Calvert, Efq.
John Calvert, Efq. jun.
Edward Calvert, Efq.
Mifs Cambell
Meff. Gainfborough and Cambell
Rev. John Carne, Nafh, &c.
Mrs. Carne, &c.
Mifs Carne, &c.
Mifs Jane Carne, &c.
Mr. Carpenter
Mifs Cafwall
Mrs. Carter, Deal, &c.
Mifs Chalié
Mrs. M. Chandler
Mr Chateau, St. Louis, Louifiana
Rev. J. Church, Rector of Flimfton
Mrs. Church
Mrs. Churchill
Mrs. Claxton
—— Claxton, Efq.
Mr. J. Cole, A. B. Jefus College, Oxford
Rev. Septimus Coilinfon, A M. Fellow of Queen's College, Oxford
Thomas Cooper, Efq. Equitable Affurance
William Cowper, Efq. Inner Temple
General Conway
Mr. Copner, &c.
Mrs. Copner, &c.
Mifs Copner, &c.
Richard Cookfey, Efq.
Mr. Thomas Cooper

Mr. Coufins
—— Cox, Efq. Swanfea
Mifs Cox
Rev. Mr. Coxe
Rev. Samuel Cote
Rev. Wm. Cooper, Clare Hall, Cambridge
VISCOUNT CREMORNE
VISCOUNTESS CREMORNE
Rev. Francis Crefwell, Clare Hall, Cambridge
Mrs. Culme
George Cure, Efq.
John Curre, Efq. &c.
Mrs. Curre, &c.
Mifs Curre
Mifs Curre, Lantwit
Mr. Cuthbert

D

Dr. Davie, Trinity College, Oxford
Rev. William Davies, Trinity College, Cambr.
Mr. Walter Davies, All Souls College, Oxford
Rev. Mr. Davies
Mr. Morgan Davies
Rev. Ed. Davies, Sodbury, 2 fets
Mr. David Davies
Mr. Oliver Davies
Wm. Davies, Efq. Court Grove

Mr.

Mr. Charles Davies
Mrs. Davies, Bath
Mifs F. Davies, Bath, &c.
Mrs. Davies
Rev. Mr. Davies, Trinity College, Cambridge
Francis Davis, Efq. Jefus College, Oxford
Rev. Wm. Davies, A. B. Jefus College, Oxford
Mrs. Day
Anthony Deane, Efq. &c.
Mrs. Deane, &c.
Mifs Deane, &c.
Mifs Rofamond Amelia Deane, &c.
Mr. Deane, All Souls College, Oxford, &c.
Rev. Mr. Deake
Rev. Mr. Deverel, Oriel College, Oxford
Mr. J. Dawkin, Chrift Church College, Oxf.
Mr. Edw. Dawkin, Magdalen College, Oxford
Reynold Tho. Deere, Efq.
John De la Bere, Efq. Cheltenham
Mrs. Denifon
EARL DELAWAR .
COUNTESS DELAWAR
LADY DINEVOR
BISHOP of DROMORE
HON. HENRY DILLON
Mrs. Sarah Dover
William Douglas, Efq. Teddington
Wm. Dowdefwell, Efq.

Robert Drummond, Efq.
Francis Douce, Efq.
Dafydd Ddu, Eryri Bardd
William Drake, Efq.
Edward Drax, Efq.
Mrs. Drax
Mrs. Mary Dunn
Theophilus Dyfon, Efq.
Mr. J. W. Dyer

E

Bryan Edwards, Efq. 6 fets
D. Baily Edwards
Mifs Edwards, Flimfton
Thomas Edwards, Efq.
Rev. Mr. Edwards
Thomas Edmondes, Efq.
Rev. Edw. Evans, Aberdare
Mrs. Evans, Ham, 3 fets
Rev. John Evans, A.M.&c.

F

LORD FALMOUTH
Mr. Fabian
Mifs Fanfliaw
Mr. Featon
Rev. —— Field, M. A.
Mr. Fielder

b 3   Mifs

Miſs Fielding
Miſs Matilda Fielding
Miſs Auguſta Fielding
Mrs. Foley
Dr. Fothergill, Bath
Rev. William Fothergill, M.A. Fellow of Queen's College, Oxford
HON. MISS FLOWER, &c.
Dr. Fox, Mark Lane
Dr. E. Long Fox, Briſtol
John Franklen, Eſq.
Thomas Franklen, Eſq.
Mrs. Freeman, Henley
Mrs. Freeman, Fawlcy Court
Mrs. Fydell

G

Rev. Dr. Gabriel
Mr. J. W. Galabin
Miſs Gardner
Meſſ. Gainſborough and Co. Bookſellers, Bath
Mrs. Gibbons
William Gibbon, Eſq.
Mr. Edmund Gill
Mrs. Mary Girardot
Dr. Glin, King's College, Cambridge, 2 ſets
Mr. Golding
Mr. Gratiot, St. Louis, Louiſiana
Amos Green, Eſq. &c.

Rev. Dr. Gregory, &c.
James Green, Eſq.
Joſeph Grote, Eſq.
Dr. Griffin
Mr. Rowland Griffiths
William Grove, Eſq. Lichfield
Thomas Gueſt, Eſq.
Miſs C. Gurney
Thynne How Gwynne, Eſq.
Mrs. Gwynne
Mr. Gwynne
Mrs. Gwynne, Bath
Rev. Samuel Gwinnett
Miſs Emilia Gwinnett, 3 ſets

H

Mr. Hamilton, Chriſt-Church College, Oxf.
Rev. John Haggitt, Fellow of Clare Hall, Cambridge, &c.
George Hardinge, Eſq. 6 ſets
Mr. William Hare, jun.
Joſeph Harford, Eſq.
Mr. J. Harriſſon, Banſtead
Mrs. Harriſſon
Mr. Thomas Harper
Miſs Fanny Harper
Mr. Hazard, Bookſeller, Bath, &c.
Mr. Henſley
Mr. Joſeph Hellier

LADY

Lady Herries
Mrs. Hervey
Miss Hillyard
Mrs. Hervey
Rev. Joseph Hoare, D. D. Principal of Jesus College. Oxford, 6 sets, &c.
Mrs. H. Hoare
William Houlston, Esq.
Mrs. Holroyd
John Hoole, Esq.
Dr. Horne, late Bishop of Norwich
Mr. Howlett
Henry Hinchcliffe, Esq. Trinity College, Camb.
Mr. Hornby, Christ-Ch. College, Oxford
Lord Howard
Rev. J. Honeywood
Mr. Corbet Hue, A. B. Fellow of Jesus Coll. Oxf.
Mr. Robert Hugh Hughs, Jesus College, Oxford
Rev. Dr. Hughs, Fellow of Jesus College, Oxf.
John Hughs, Esq. Bath
John Hughes, Esq. Wrexham
Dafydd ap Huw, Bardd
Herbert Hurst, Esq.
Rowland Hunt, Esq.
Mrs. Hunt
John Hunt, Esq. 5 sets
Rev. Dr. Hunt, All Souls College, Oxford
Wm. Hunt, Esq. Charlton
Mrs. I. Hunter
Mrs. Hunt

Mrs. Hyet
Miss Hygon, Cheltenham

I and J

Rev. Dr. Jackson, Dean of Christ Church, Oxford, 2 sets
Mrs. Jackson
Charles James, Esq.
Miss James
Citoyen Janſen, Imprimeur & Libraire, Cloitre St. Honoré, Paris
Rev. Humphrey Jeston
Lewis Jenkins, Esq.
Mr. George Jenkins, A. B. Jesus College, Oxford
Earl of Ilchester
Mr. J. Johnson, Bookseller, St. Paul's Ch. Yard, &c.
Sir William Jones, Bt.
Calvert Rich. Jones, Esq.
Valentine Jones, Esq.
T. P. Jones, Esq.
Theophilus Jones, Esq.
Robert Jones, Esq. Fonmon Castle
Rev. Evan Jones
Rev. Mr. Jones, Curate of Flimston, &c.
Mr. Morgan Jones
Capt. W. Jones, Waterford
Daniel Jones, Esq.
Mr. Edw. Jones, B. T. C.
Rev. Henry Jones, M. A.
Miss Jones, Lisworney
Rev.

Rev. J. Jones, Bletchley
Rev. *J. Jones*, A. B. Fellow of Jesus College, Oxford
Thomas Jones, Esq.
Mr. Owen Jones, 6 sets, &c.
Mrs. Isted, Bath
Mrs. Iremonger
Rev. *Peter Julian*, A. B. Jesus College, Oxford
Rev. Hugh Jones, Lewisham
Mr. Tho. Jones, Y Bardd Cloff
Rev. D. Jones, Hackney College
Mr. Edward Johns
Mr. Edward Jones, *Môn*
Mr. Owen Jones, *Môn*
James Jones, Esq. New York
Dr. Samuel Jones, Lower Dublin, Pennsylvania
Mr. Incledon

K

Mrs. Keate
Mrs. Kennicott
Rev. Dr. Kent
Mrs. Kemeys
Mr. Kinder
Edward King, Esq.
Mr. King, Statuary, Bath
Rev. *Dr. Kippis, &c.*

Mr. *Kitson*, &c.
—— *Knight*, Esq.
Mrs Knight
Rev. Mr. Knight
Rev. *Vicesimus Knox*, D.D.
Miss Knox

L

Bishop of Landaff
Rev. Benjamin Latrobe
Mr. Langton
Mrs. Langton
Miss Diana Langton
Rev. *Dr. Layard*, Prebendary of Worcester
Edward Lewis, Esq.
Miss Lee, Bath, &c.
Sir John Leicester
Rev. *Mr. Leicester*
Dr. Lettsom
Thomas Lewis, Esq.
Richard Lewis, Esq.
Rev. Francis Lewis
Mrs. Lewis, Crick House
Rev. *H. Llewellin*, Fellow of Jesus College, Oxf.
Edmund Lechmere, Esq.
Miss Lewis
John Leigh, Esq.
John Lewis, B. A. Fellow of Jesus College, Oxf.
Mr. Wm. Lewis, Fellow of Jesus College, Oxf.
John Llewellin, Esq. Ynys y Gerwyn, 3 sets

· John

John Llewellin, Efq. Welfh St. Donats .
Mrs. Llewellin, Caftelle
Mrs. Light, Bath
Wadham Lock, Efq.
Mrs. Lockwood
Mrs. Long
Mifs Long
Thomas Lowfield, Efq.
Major Lord
Mrs. Lord
Rev. Richard Lloyd, Hay
David Edward Lewis Lloyd, Efq.
Mr. William Lloyd, Jefus College, Oxford
Mr. John Lloyd .
Mr. Joseph Lloyd, Book-feller, Briftol
Robert St. John Lucas, Efq.

M

Sir Herbert Mackworth, 2 fets
Digby Mackworth, Efq.
Mrs. Digby Mackworth
Mrs. Jane Mackworth
Lady Macleod
Thomas Maningham, Efq.
Mr. Marfan &c.
Jofeph May, Efq.
Edward May, Efq. jun.
Thomas Markham, Efq.

Mr. Marfhall, Bookfeller, Bath, &c.
Rev. Wm. Lort Manfel, Public Orator of Camb. Univ.
Wm. Matthews, Efq. Bath, &c.
H. *Marfh*, Statuary, Briftol
William Marfden, Efq.
Rev W. Mafon, York
Mrs. Mafon
Mr. Wm. Maltby
Mr. Jofeph Maurice
William Melmoth, Efq. Bath, &c.
Mr. Meyler, Bookfeller, Bath, &c.
Mrs. Meyrick
Henry Simpfon Michell, Efq.
Mifs Michell
Mr. Thomas Minfhull, A.B. Jefus College, Oxford
—— Molend, Efq.
—— Monk, Efq.
Rev. Ifaac Monkhoufe, A.M. Fellow of Queen's College, Oxford
Mrs. Montagu, 12 fets, &c.
Mifs Hannah More, &c.
Mr. More, Chrift Church, Oxford
Rev. John Morgan, &c.
Mrs. Morgan, Cowbridge
John Morgan, Efq. Tredegar, 3 fets, &c.
Mr. Watkin Morgan
Mr.

3

Mr. William Morgan

Rev. Dr. Morgan, Jesus College

Rev. N. Morgan, Bath

Rev. Edward Morgan, B.D. Fellow of Jesus College, Oxford, &c.

Rev. Thos. Morgan, A. B. of ditto

Mr. John Morgan, St. Athans

Rev. John Morgan, St. Mary Hill

Rev. Richard Morgan, Reculver

Wm. Morgan, Esq. Equitable Assurance Office

Edward Morgan, Esq. Cardiff

Miss Caroline Morris, &c.

Mr. William Morrice

Mrs. Morris

Miss Murray

Mrs. Mytton

N

Mrs. Naper, Slaughter, Gloucester

Miss Nettleship, Cheltenham, &c.

William Nettleship, Esq.

HON. MISS NEVILL, &c.

Rev. J. Nicholl, Remenham, &c.

HON. MRS. NICHOLI, &c.

Rev. Rob. Nicholl, A. M.

William Nicholl, Esq. &c.

Mrs. Nicholl

Mrs. Nicholl, Ham, &c.

Mr. Deputy Nichols, &c.

Rev. Mr. Ninds

Samuel Norman, Esq.

BISHOP of NORWICH

Rev. Dr. Nowell, Principal of St. Mary's Hall, Ox.

Mrs. Nowell

Mrs. Nugent

O

Rev. Mr. Owen, Upton Scudamore

Thomas Owen, Esq. Waterford

Mr. Wm. Owen, &c.

Mrs. Owen, &c.

Aneurin Owen

Mr. John Owen, Bookseller 6 sets

Titus Owen, Esq.

Miss Nancy Owen

Mr. Ord

Mrs.

Mrs. Ord
Miſs Ord
LORD ORFORD, 3 ſets
Mr. Oſwald, Paris

P

—— Paine, Eſq. Secretary to the Prince of Wales
Mr. Thomas Paine
Paul Panton, Eſq. Angleſea
Paul Panton, jun. Eſq. Lincoln's Inn
Rev. Dr. Parr
Rev. Robert Parry, B. D. Fellow of St. John's College, Cambridge
Dr. Parry, Phyſician, Bath, &c
Mr. Parſons
Mr. Richard Pearſon
LADY JULIANA PENN
JOHN PENN, Eſq.
Thomas Pennant, Eſq. 6 ſets
Rev. Dr. Penny
Rev. Dr. Peckard, Maſter of Magdalen College, Cambridge
Jaſper Peck, Eſq.
Chriſt. Pegge, M.D. Oxf.
Mrs. Pegge

Rev. Thomas Phelps, A.B. Jeſus College, Oxford
Evan Phillips, Eſq. Caſtletown, &c.
Richard Turberville Picton, Eſq.
HIS EXCELLENCY THOMAS PINCKNEY, Miniſter Plenipotentiary from the United States of America
Mrs. Piozzi
John Popkin, Eſq. &c.
Mrs. Popkin, &c.
Rev. Gervas Powell, LL.B. &c.
Mr. Charles Powell, Jeſus College, Oxford, &c.
Gabriel Powell, Eſq. Swanſea
Governor Pownall, 4 ſets, &c.
Mrs. Pownall
HON.THOMAS POWNALL, Quebec
Rev. T. Powys, &c.
Mr. Powys
Mrs. Powys
Rev. Dr. Prieſtley, &c.
Rice Price, Eſq. Cowbridge
Rev. Dr. Price, Hereford
Rev. Dr. Price, late of Hackney
Dr. Price, Glamorgan
Charles Price, Eſq Newport
John Price, Eſq. Bath

Mrs.

Mrs. Price, Landaff
Rev. John Price, Bodleian
Library, 2 sets, &c.
Mr. John Price, Merchant
Mr. Samuel Price, Apo-
thecary, Fore Street
Edmund Probyn, Esq.
Mr. Proper, Bristol
Henry James Pye, Esq. &c.
Mrs. Bathurst Pye

Q

Mr. Ambrose Quarman,
Keynsham

R

Robert Raikes, Esq. Glou-
cester
Mr. John Rannie
Rev. Mr. Rankin, Ken-
tucky
Rev. Mr Randolph
Mrs. Randall
Miss Ramsden
Miss Ratcliffe
Jeremiah Redwood, Esq.
Philip Redwood, Esq. Ja-
maica

Mr. Owen Rees, Booksel-
ler, Bristol
Rev. Josiah Rees, Gelli-
gron
Mr. John Rees, Jesus Col-
lege, Oxford
Rev. Morgan Rees
Rev. Mr. Richards, Oriel
College, Oxford
Rev. Mr. Richards, Rec-
tor of Farnborough
Samuel Richardson, Esq.
Mr. Ricketts, Statuary,
Bath, &c.
Mr. John Ricketts, Sta-
tuary
Miss Ricketts
Rev. Robert Rickards
John Richards, Esq. City
Road
Mr. James Robins, Ja-
maica
Miss Robins, ditto
BISHOP OF ROCHESTER
Colonel Rodd, &c.
Miss F. Rosser
Major General Rooke
Mrs. Rooper
Miss Rodbard
Rev. John Roberts, B. D.
Jesus College, Oxford
Mr. Rowlands, A. B.
Jesus College, Oxford
Samuel Rogers, Esq. &c.
Mr. Thomas Rowland, Sta-
tuary, Bristol
Mr. David Roberts, India
House

LORD

LORD ROMNEY
LADY ROTHES
Mr. R. Rofe
Mr. J. Rouffeau

S

Robert Salufbury, Efq.
    Lanwern
John Salufbury, Efq.
Rev. Mr. Thelwall Saluf-
    bury
Rev. Lynch Salufbury
Charles Sackville, Efq. 5
    fets
David Samwell, Efq. &c.
Rev. Mr. Sandford, B. D.
    Fellow of Jefus Col-
    lege, Oxford
Mifs Anna Seward,
    Ofyddes ym mraint
    Beirdd Ynys Prydain,
    &c.
William Seward, Efq. &c.
Rev. Mr. Seys
Mrs. Scot, &c.
Mrs. Scot, Bottalog Mei-
    rion
Alexander Scot, Efq.
Robert Scott, Efq.
Mrs. Scott

Sutton Sharpe, Efq.
Granville Sharpe, Efq. &c.
Ralph Sheldon, Efq.
    Swanfea
Jofeph Shrimpton, Efq.
Mr. Robert Sidney, A. B.
    Jefus College, Oxford
Rev. Mr. Simpfon, Fellow
    of Univerfity College,
    Oxford
Denham Skeet, LL. D.
Mr. Thomas Stackboufe,
    Statuary
Mrs, Stead
Mr. Stone
George Smith, Efq. Pierce-
    field, &c.
Mrs. Smith, ditto, &c.
—— Smith, M. D. Bath
Mifs Smith, Cooper's Hill
Mr. John Smith
Captain Sotheby
Mr. Sotheby
Mifs Sotheby
Mr. Gilead Spencer, Ja-
    maica
Henry Stephens, Efq.
    Chavenage Houfe,
    Gloucefter, 2 fets
Mrs. Stephens, 2 fets
Mifs Martha Sutton
Mifs Sarah Sutton
LORD SUDLEY
Mrs. Surters

T Thomas

T

Thomas Manſel Talbot,
  Eſq. 3 ſets
Mr. J. Tayler
Mrs. Anne Taylor
Philip Thickneſſe, Eſq.
David Thomas, Eſq.
David Thomas, jun. Eſq.
Miſs Mary Thomas
Edward Thomas, Eſq.
Robert Thomas, Eſq. Pem-
  broke College, Oxford
Thomas Thomas, A. B. Je-
  ſus College, Oxford
Rev. Wm. Thomas, Chan-
  cellor of the Cathedral
  of Landaff
Miſs Mary Thomas, Lis-
  worney, &c.
Rev. Joſhua Thomas,
  Leominſter
N. Thompſon, Eſq.
C. Throckmorton, M. D.
Rev. Robert Thornton
John Toke, Eſq.
John Horne Tooke, Eſq.
  &c.
J. P. Towry, Eſq.

William Toulmin, Eſq.
  Hackney
LADY BRIDGET TOLLE-
  MACHE
John Towgood, Eſq. 2 ſets
William Towgood, Eſq.
  2 ſets
Edmund Traherne, Eſq.
Llewellin Traherne, Eſq.
Captain Trigge
Edmund Tyrwhitt, Eſq.

V

LORD VERNON
John Vaughan, Eſq. Gol-
  den Grove, &c.
Griffith Vaughan, Eſq. Je-
  ſus College, Oxford
Mr. Vaughan
Mr. M. Viel
Mrs. Vigor

W HU-

W

HUMANITY'S WILBERFORCE

GENERAL WASHING-
TON
Robert Watfon Wade,
Efq.
—— Wade, Efq.
Fowler Walker, Efq.
Mrs. Wall
Rev. Mr. Wall, Merton
College, Oxford
Mr. S. Ward
Mrs. Walters, Ruthyn, &c.
Mifs Walters, Ruthyn, &c.
Rev. John Walters, Lan-
dough, &c.
Mr. Henry Walters, Book-
feller, Cowbridge
Rev. John Walters, Frome
Mr. Watfon, Saville Row
Rev. Thomas Wells, B. D.
Fellow of Worcefter
College, Oxford
Mrs. Weddal, &c.
Samuel Whitchurch, Efq.
Stephen White, Efq.
Mrs. White
Mifs Lydia White, &c.
William White, Efq.
Rev. Mr. Whaley, 2 fets
Mr. Wilbraham, Chrift
Church, Oxford, 2 fets
Thomas Wilkins, Efq.

Mr. Edward Wilkins,
Lantwit
Rev. Mr. Willis
Rev. Mr. Williams, Mafter
of Cowbridge Free-
School, &c.
Rev. George Williams,
Lantrithyd
Rev. Dr. Williams, Sy-
denham, &c.
Mrs. Williams, ditto, &c.
Rev. Mr. Williams, Mar-
gam
Mifs Williams, Lifworney
Mr. W. Williams
Bloom Williams, Efq.
Henry Wilmot, Efq. &c.
Mrs. Wilmot, &c.
John Wilmot, Efq. &c.
Edward Wilmot, Efq.
Mrs. Wilmot
Mr. Henry Porter Wilfon,
&c.
Thomas Williams, Sculp-
tor, Jamaica
Miles Williams, Brick-
layer, Jamaica
John Williams, Brick-
layer, Jamaica
Mr. E. Williams, Book-
feller, Strand, 6 fets
Mr.

Mr. *Thomas Williams*,
Bookseller, Leadenhall
Street, 6 sets
Mr. J. Williams, Bardd
Penllyn
Mr. J. Williams, Bardd
St. Athan, &c.
Rev. Peter Williams
Taliesin Williams, Flim-
ston
Miss Peggy Williams,
Flimston
Miss Ann Matthews Wil-
liams, Flimston
Edward Williams, senior,
Flimston
John Williams, Esq. Dyf-
fryn
Walter Wiltshire, Esq &c.
Mr. Wood, A. B. Christ
Church, Oxford
Rev. Elhanan Winchester
Mrs. Winford
Miss Winford

Mr. James Woodhouse
MARQUIS of WORCESTER
MARCHIONESS of WOR-
CESTER
Rob. Wrixon, Esq. Oriel
College, Oxford
Thomas Wyndham, Esq. 3
sets
Mrs. Wyndham. 3 sets
SIR WATKIN WILLIAMS
WYNNE, Bart. 2 sets,
&c.

Y

Mrs. Yearsly, Bristol

P O E M S.

T O L A U D A N U M.

I.

WHILST, crowding on my woful hour,

Fate's deep'ning glooms indignant low'r,

    And crush my wearied foul ;

Thou, *Laudanum*, can'ft quickly fteep

My burning eyes in balmy fleep,

    And ev'ry grief controul.

2.

When Reafon ftrives, but ftrives in vain,
To banifh care, to vanquifh pain,
        And calm fad thoughts to reft ;
Thy foothing virtues can impart
A bland fenfation to my heart,
        And heal my wounded breaft.

3..

Whilft fell Difeafe, with rapid flame,
Preys ireful on my feeble frame,
        Pervading ev'ry vein ;
Thou canft repel the venom'd rage,
The fever'd anguifh canft affuage,
        ·And blunt the tooth of Pain.

4.

When wakeful Senfibility
Her wrongs recounts, I fly to thee,
        And feel her touch no more ;

At

At painful Memory's loud call,

'Twas she, with fingers dipt in gall,

My rankling bosom tore.

5.

With foul-corroding thought opprefs'd,

Whilst keen affliction fills my breast,

And swells the tide of grief;

O! shed thy balm into my heart,

And, plucking thence the piercing dart,

Bestow thy kind relief.

6.

Now Comfort shuns my woful fight,

And sad returns the sleeplefs night,

In sable glooms array'd;

I court thy pow'rs with anxious mind,

And, on the down of rest reclin'd,

I blefs thy lenient aid.

7. My

7.

My joyleſs hours I waſte alone,
Unpitied weep, unheeded moan,
    Unfriended ſigh forlorn;
Conſign to grief my crawling years,
The victim of deſponding cares,
    Exiſting but to mourn.

8.

Thou faithful friend in all my grief,
In thy ſoft arms I find relief;
    In thee forget my woes:
Unfeeling waſte my wint'ry day,
And paſs with thee the night away,
    Reclin'd in ſoft repoſe.

9.

O! ſtill exert thy ſoothing pow'r,
Till fate leads on the welcom'd hour,
    To bear me hence away;

To

To where purfues no ruthlefs foe,

No feeling keen awakens woe,

    No faithlefs friends betray.

RURAL

RURAL INCIDENTS.

A LYRIC PASTORAL.

1.

WHEN early primrofes appear,
　And vales are deck'd with daffodils,
I hail the new-reviving year,
　And foothing hope my bofom fills;
The lambkin bleating on the plain,
　The fwallow feen with gladden'd eye,
The welcom'd cuckoo's merry ftrain,
　Proclaim the joyful fummer nigh.

2.

The ploughman whiftling o'er the lea,
　The clacking of yon diftant mill,
The throftle on the budding tree,
　The tow'ring fkylark's early trill;

The

The whifpers of the weftern breeze,

   The prattling brook that winds along;

Such fylvan founds my fancy pleafe,

   Supply my theme of rural fong.

3.

The fruitful orchard's lovely bloom,

   Now ufhers in the fprightly May;

The fkies have loft their wint'ry gloom,

   The chilly gales are flown away;

Returning nightingales appear,

   And charm with fong the midnight hour;

And I, their melting notes to hear,

   Frequent my lone, fequefter'd bow'r.

4.

Well-pleas'd I view the lowing herds

   That wanton in the clover'd vale;

And, lift'ning to the choral birds,

   The balm of healthful fkies inhale;

Health!

Health! lovely darling of my foul,

    I feek thy paths with anxious heed;

For thee reject the mantling bowl,

    And on the dairy's nectar feed.

5.

When golden Morn's refulgent rays

    Give luftre to the dewy vale,

Whilft June its rofy bloom difplays,

    And eglantines perfume the gale;

Let me fome lonely dell frequent,

    And give a loofe to glowing thought,

And meditate with warm intent,

    The tuneful verfe with fancy fraught.

6.

With fhepherds on the thymy down,

    I love to pafs the fummer's day,

Or trace (and mark the privet blown)

    The fhady thicket's winding way;

Be thou, my lovely Delia, there,
   And walk with me the brake along,
I'll sing to pleafe thy partial ear,
   Whilft love infpires th'impaffion'd fong.

7.

When lads and laffes, making hay,
   Chat mirthful in the verdant mead,
I form for them the fportive lay,
   Or pipe upon my rural reed;
With rake in hand I often walk,
   With them along the new-mown vale,
And cheer the fwains with merry talk,
   And pleafe the nymphs with am'rous tale.

8.

When reapers to the golden field,
   Hie blithfome in the buftling morn,
I rear the fhock, or fickle wield,
   And, gladden'd, view the ripen'd corn;

B 5

Now, lift'ning to the rural Wit,

    I join the laugh of loud applaufe,

Or tofs aloft the frothy cit,

    That dares tranfgrefs our harveft laws..

9.

In wealthful Autumn's ev'ning fair,

    When all the corn is gather'd in,

I to the ruftic rout repair,

    And help to fwell the cheerful din:

We, that in rural toils have join'd,

    Now at the farmer's board regale ;

The feaft enjoy with gleeful mind,

    And pufh about the nut-brown ale.

10.

The treafures of the cultur'd field,

    Are in our barns with caution ftor'd ;

The racy fruits our orchards yield,

    Heap up the winter's ample hoard ;

The

The balmy fweets of toiling bees,

    Collected are with careful hand ;

We fet our anxious minds at eafe,

    For Plenty revels in the land.

11.

When favour'd by the fcentful morn,

    I trace thick woods, or climb the rocks,

Urge on the chace with hound and horn,

    And far purfue the wily fox;

His nightly ravage in the fold,

    The fhepherd fhall no longer dread,

Acclaiming fwains fhall foon behold,

    The caitiff number'd with the dead.

12.

The lawns have loft their vivid hue,

    No flow'rets bloom, no lambkins bleat ;

Yet with rejoicing eyes we view

    The verdure of the fpringing wheat :

Revolving

Revolving Plenty ·buds around,

   It fhall our future wealth difpenfe; '

We 'll hedge with care the precious ground,

   And truft it then to Providence.

13.

Now dark December's tempeft rends

   The frowning fkies with dreadful ire,

And, chatting with my jocund friends,

   I fit befide the blazing fire:

Your herds now fhiver in the mead,

   Ye fwains, their urgent calls obey;

Their fteps to timely fhelter lead,

   And deal around the fragrant hay.

14.

Contending ftorms now rage around,

   With fnow the fields are cover'd o'er;

Huge billows break with frightful found,

   And roll their terrors to the fhore;

Now Nature feels a sore decay,

We to the mournful scene attend,

So pass our checquer'd years away,

And in the grave our bustles end.

———————————

S T A N Z A S

WRITTEN IN

L O N D O N IN 1773.

I.

WHEN the bright morn of life appears
     In retrofpective view,
I mournful dwell on vernal years,
When time, unmark'd by galling cares,
     On wings of pleafure flew.

2.

O blifsful hours! ere led aftray
     By Fame's alluring tale;
When Reafon's undifputed fway,
Could ev'ry wayward thought allay;
     Could o'er my heart prevail.

3. Why,

3.

Why, *Cambria*, did I quit thy fhore ?

The fcenes I lov'd fo dear ;

With wounded feelings ranking fore,.

I languifh, and thy lofs deplore,

In Folly's hateful fphere.

4.

Dear native land ! though thoughtlefs Pride

Contemns thy peaceful plains,

By Virtue's energy fupply'd,

The joys of Nature ftill abide

Amongft thy cheerful fwains.

5.

Sad Memory recalls the day,

When o'er thy lawns alone,

Exploring Fancy's mazy way,

My Mufe firft tried her infant lay,

Made firft her efforts known.

6. Ap-

6.

Applauded by th' unletter'd ſwain,

She felt her pinions grow ;

She pleas'd the beauties of the plain,

Whilſt Nature bade her ſimple ſtrain

In artleſs numbers flow.

7.

Thus, in *Glamorgan's* happy land,

I ſpent my blifsful time ;

My rural ſonnet playful plann'd,

The novel charm of Nature ſcann'd,

New ſubjeét of my rhyme.

8.

Glamorgan, boaſt thy ſky ſerene ;

Thy health-infpiring gales ;

Thy funny plains luxuriant green ;

Thy graceful mountains' airy ſcene ;

Their wild romantic vales.

9. With

9.

With Nature's wealth fupremely bleft ;

With peace, with plenty crown'd ;

In thy *white cots* *, a cheerful gueft,

Pure Joy dilates the glowing breaft,

And Gladnefs fmiles around.

10. Re-

---

* *In thy white cots.*] It has, from very remote antiquity, been the cuftom in *Glamorgan* to white-wafh the houfes, not only the infides, but the outfides alfo ; and even the barns, ftables, walls of yards, gardens, &c. In a very ancient poem, by fome attributed to *Aneurin,* who lived about the year 550, we have the following paffage :

> Gnawd ym Morganwg ddïwg ddynion,
> A Gwragedd mewn mawredd a muriau gwynion.

> In *Glamorgan* the people are courteous and gentle,
> Married women are honoured, and the walls are white.

Dafydd ab Gwilym, a bard that flourifhed about 1350, fays of *Glamorgan,*

> E gâr Bardd y wlâd bardd bonn,
> A'i gwinoedd a'i thai gwynion.

The

10.

Receive thy Bard! he fpeeds again,
  With truth-replenifh'd mind,
To range once more thy humble plain,
And pafs through life a rural fwain,
  To Heav'ns high will refign'd.

11. O,

The Bard loves this beautiful country, its wines, and its white houfes.

And in another place, invoking the Sun, he fays,

  Tefeg fore, gwnâ r llî'n llonn,
  Ag annerch y tai gwynion.

Thou Sun of the bright morning, beam joyfulnefs around; and falute the white houfes of *Glamorgan.*

Deio ab Ieuan Du, a Bard that wrote about 1450, fays,

  Morganwg muriau gwynion.

  Glamorgan of the white walls.

But it would be endlefs to quote all the Bards who have noticed this cuftom, which ftill continues.

Mr.

11.

O, *London!* let me turn away

 From thee my fadden'd eyes;

With drooping foul, to grief a prey,

Long have I fpent the joylefs day,

 Beneath thy tainted fkies.

12.

To trace thy fcenes, why did I long

 To dwell with baleful art;

Turn fool to pleafe thy worthlefs throng,

Affect thy vice, and forely wrong

 The feelings of my heart?

Mr. Penruddocke Wyndham, in his Tour through *Monmouthfhire and Wales in the year* 1781, fays, that in Glamorgan " the houfes, walls, and out-buildings, are commonly white- " wafhed; and there is fcarcely a cottage to be feen, which is " not regularly brufhed over every month." P. 37, 2d edit.

Mr. Strutt, from *Diodorus Siculus,* fays, that the *Britons* white-wafhed their houfes with chalk (Chronicle of England, p. 254). From hence it appears that the Welfh of *Glamorgan* ftill retain a very ancient Britifh cuftom.

13. See

13.

See Fafhion to thy dazzled crowd
 Her gaudy plumes difplay ;
Mad vot'ries of her tinfel proud,
Raife their tyrannic fhouts aloud,
 And urge her fov'reign fway.

14.

How throngs around her giddy train,
 Blind to the charms of truth ;
Vice loudly chaunts her fyren ftrain ;
Exerts her wily fkill to gain
 The unexperienced youth.

15.

Think not, meek child of innocence,
 Thy truth a merit here ;
Thy blamelefs manners give offence,
And coxcomb cits will recompenfe
 Thy virtues with a fneer.

16. Thou

16.

Thou muſt approach vile Folly's throne;
 Reluctantly be vain;
Thy conſcious innocence diſown;
Affect, and boaſt, a vice unknown;
 A guilt unpractiſed feign.

17.

Yet, would'ſt thou call her glories thine,
 Tear conſcience from thy heart;
With fair pretence, and deep deſign,
Go act, or never hope to ſhine,
 Unfeign'd the villain's part.

18.

Whilſt envied Virtue nobly warms
 Thy yet unconquer'd mind,
Fly from her vile, polluting arms;
Nor gaze on meretricious charms;
 Nor caſt one look behind.

19.

O fly! nor let thy gen'rous heart,
  Submit to her controul:
She'll foon find out its weakeft part;
Will haunt thee with infidious art,
  And fafcinate thy foul.

20.

Bright Reafon! 'twas thy pow'rful hand
  Preferv'd me from the fnare,
From fchemes by fell Temptation plann'd;
I heard thy call, thy mild command,
  And blefs'd thy guardian care.

21.

Whilft toiling on life's ruffled fea,
  'Gainft adverfe Fortune's tide,
Amid the ftorm I call to thee,
Thou, heav'nly monitor, fhalt be
  My comfort and my guide.

22.

And thou, whofe will the Heav'ns obey,
 With Love's eternal awe,
Led ftill by thy celeftial ray,
Bid me through life's eventful day,
 Live ftudious of thy law.

———————

CASTLES

CASTLES IN THE AIR.

WRITTEN IN 1777.

———— *The baseless fabric of a vision.*

SHAKSPEARE.

M Y lot in life, nor blame I fate,

Unborn to title or estate,

Was to procure a slender stock,

By building *houses* on the *rock*;

Blest Providence! for ever kind,

Gave me a truth-discerning mind;

Did to this mind the pow'rs impart,

Of useful skill and honest art;

And, Pride's intrusion to prevent,

Gave humbled thoughts of calm content.

4   Toil's

Toil's healthful hand with eafe acquir'd

Whate'er my bridled wifh defir'd;

All Nature's wants were well fupplied,

Nature, with little fatisfied;

Peace crown'd the labours of my day,

No thorns beftrew'd my fhelter'd way:

No charms of foul-corrupting gold,

Vile price for peace and virtue fold,

Could e'er my cautious mind employ;

Reafon difclaim'd the guilty joy.

   Pow'rs, known too late, with Nature dwell,

In Frailty's night-envelop'd cell,

Caftled in Error's murky cloud,

Where lawlefs Paffion ftorms aloud;

Mad Folly there, with varied wiles,

Youth's unfufpecting foul beguiles;

Thence came that frantic elf Defire,

On rapid pinions plum'd with fire;

Clad in the borrow'd hues of light,

A Syren lovely to the fight;

She tuned her thought-relaxing lay,

And led my captiv'd soul away.

I felt ftrange pains, unknown before,

And filenc'd Reafon rul'd no more;

A dulcet grief, a pleafing fmart,

Diftrefs'd at once, and charm'd my heart;

Bewilder'd rants employ'd my tongue;

I often figh'd, and often fung;

Was oft by Fancy's gloom o'ercaft:

'Twas Love, mad Love, I found at laft.

Tranfported with th' inchanting name,

Fool, I began to feed the flame;

Told Celia, that my bleeding breaft

Felt all her charms, and knew no reft;

Told her my paffion was fincere;

And witnefs'd this with many a tear.

Now Celia play'd a fkilful part,

And fported with my love-fick heart;

A mutual paffion fhe confefs'd,

I thought myfelf now truly bleft;

My

My joys were full; my cares were flown;

For Celia, sure, was now my own;

How bleſt the life with Celia ſpent,

In tender love, and ſweet content.

 Alas! young *Tinſel*, blithe and gay,

A boaſting warrior, came that way;

She ſaw the glitt'ring *Hero* come,

With ſound of trumpet, beat of drum;

She heard him prate, admir'd his coat;

'Tis on ſuch trifles women doat.

Tinſel addreſs'd my fickle fair,

And read the lover's common prayer;

Play'd with ſucceſs the coxcomb's part,

And ſtole from me my Celia's heart.

Celia now yields to new deſires;

A brighter flame her ſoul inſpires;

The peaceful maſon baniſh'd far,

She weds th' enſanguin'd ſon of war.

Behold, exulting! now they come,

Attended by the noiſy drum;

High-

High-fqueaking fife's harfh accents play,

To celebrate the joyful day.

My fighs I check, nor once upbraid;

For, fure, I loft a worthlefs maid;

Whofe heart was never form'd to prove

The blifs refin'd of conftant love.

How often has my anxious mind

With Celia's love all blifs combin'd;

Promis'd all pleafures in her fmile;

Joys that could ev'ry care beguile.

How bleft! what happinefs divine!

To call the lovely charmer mine.

Thus, bootlefs, toil'd my bufy heart;

Warm fancies thrill'd in ev'ry part;

And, after all its labours paft,

'Twas difappointed thus at laft;

Hopes, that I nurs'd with wiftful care,

Were only *Caftles built in air*;

Tow'rs, where I thought with peace to dwell,

But, ruin'd foon, they downward fell,

I felt

I felt a momentary ſhock,

But landed ſafe on Reaſon's *rock*.

And now, by all that 's good, I ſwore,

Woman ſhould trick my heart no more ;

Friendſhip could ſoothe my cares to reſt,

Should reign ſole monarch of my breaſt ;

My ſoul, with all it's warmth inſpire,

Whilſt Reaſon fann'd the hallow'd fire,

Rous'd up in ev'ry glowing ſenſe

The fervors of Benevolence :

To crown my wiſh, I found a few,

Whoſe hearts, I thought, were ſound and true ,

Compeers, of ſeeming worth poſſeſs'd ;

I thoſe with utmoſt warmth careſs'd ;

Gave up to thoſe my thoughtleſs heart,

Wide-opening ev'ry ſecret part ;

Baniſh'd Suſpicion, that vile elf,

And meaſur'd others by myſelf:

Deteſting views of ſordid wealth,

My time, my labour, and my health,

Were

Were facrific'd to ferve my friend;

I gain'd in this my ftudied end;

I knew fuccefs a little while,

Saw Fortune on my labours fmile;

Could often, from a fcanty ftore,

Afford a penny to the poor,

That bore Misfortune's galling load,

In fad Affliction's thorny road.

The fons of Cunning fang my praife,

Well-fkill'd in Flatt'ry's wily ways;

A well-feign'd gratitude exprefs'd;

I ne'er perceiv'd 'twas all a jeft.

When Flatt'ry plies her guileful art,

Alas! how falls th' unweeting heart;

With confcious rectitude elate,

No fnare difcovers till too late.

Thus, thoughtlefs pafs'd my fummer's day,,

Till all my pence were flown away!

Chill Penury returns at laft:

I fhiver in her wint'ry blaft;

Dull

Dull purfe-proud clowns, *rejoicing*, note
My fcanty meal, my thread-bare coat;
Now fall away my *prudent* friends,
Ah ! nought remains to ferve their ends;
All chang'd, they now confpire to blame;
All join to vilify my name;
With alter'd look infult: and thofe
I ferv'd the moft, were moft my foes;
Of faults, unpractifed faults accus'd;
By *knaves*, by *fools*, my name abus'd;
Wealth to th' approving crowd harangu'd,
Said I was poor, and why not hang'd?
Such was the crime, well-prov'd on me;
Th' enormous guilt of Poverty.

What art thou, Friendfhip, but a found?
A fhade in wilder'd fancies found;
Deception's lab'rinth, blindly trac'd
Through life's inhofpitable wafte;
Thy golden domes, that feem'd fo fair,
Were only *Caftles built in air*;

From

From whence, a ruin'd heap around,

They fell, and crush'd me to the ground.

　　Mirth saw my wrongs, and took my part;

She promis'd raptures to my heart;

Weil-tutor'd in her smirking school,

I learn'd to laugh at knave and fool;

And Innocence, with peaceful breast,

Can laugh and sing, though sore deprefs'd.

Now Satire came, with fi'ry pow'rs;

· Engag'd my thoughts; employ'd my hours;

She feather'd Truth's unerring dart,

And flung it at the rascal's heart;

Opening to view that dark retreat,

Where nestled villainy complete;

Pleas'd, I beheld the writhing elf,

Wild—agonizing in himself;

Pale madden'd looks the sting confess'd,

That furious tore his conscious breast;

Whilst, at his pain, th' observing crowd

Rais'd the sarcastic laugh aloud;

For

For ev'ry knave will worry down
A neighbour's vice, but not his own.

  Dead midnight reigns, and all around
Lock'd in th' embrace of sleep profound;
Save where yon Bacchanalian voice
Bids many a thoughtless fool rejoice;
I thither fly, and bear along,
The chorus of his frantic song;
Mad Riot roars, it's language fraught
With jest obscene, with brutal thought;
Folly commands, and all obey,
'Till from yon East the golden ray
Beams on these hooting owls of night,
Who, stagg'ring, fly th' upbraiding light;
And seek the sot's polluted bed,
To lay the fume-encumber'd head;
There waste, in beastly snores, away
The genial hours of cheerful day.

  Unruly Mirth, no more of thee;
Thou nurse of rude brutality;

Vil·

Vile waſter of the days of youth ;

Mad ſcoffer at the laws of Truth ;

Great hard'ner of the human breaſt,

Be thine the dull unmeaning jeſt ;

Speak out, and gain thy worthleſs end ;

Nor fear thy God, nor ſpare thy friend ;

Enjoy thy triumphs, and deſpiſe

All that can charm the good and wiſe ;

The ſtupid laugh, th' immoral ſong,

To thee, to thee alone, belong ;

I flew to thee from rankling care,

But found *thy* caſtles *built in air :*

Thy vile enjoyments canker'd all,

Thy ſpurious pleaſures drench'd in gall.

  Bright Wiſdom calls, I will obey,

Will ſeek and trace her flow'ry way ;

Her paths of pleaſantneſs and peace,

Strew'd with true joys that never ceaſe ;

She ſhall inſtruct my willing heart,

And all her ſacred lore impart :

I   She

She fhall beftow thofe pure delights

Of guiltlefs days, and peaceful nights ;

Calm thoughts on Truth's plain maxims bent,

Heav'n's ample fource of rich content.

Thus will I fpend my fpan of life,

Well-fhelter'd from the ftorms of ftrife;

Improve my heart on Virtue's plan,

And do to all what good I can;

Nor aught, incautious, take in hand,

Till confcious Duty gives command ;

Till feen in Truth's meridian light,

The dictates of eternal Right.

'Tis true, this weak unftable heart

May from its path a moment ftart;

Some rebel paffion may controul,

A little while, th' unguarded foul :

The foot of Nature, now and then,

May flip ; but fhe will rife again ;

Will to her aid Religion call,

To guard her from a fecond fall;

And *knaves* may blame, and *fools* may mock;

But this is building on the *rock* *.

---

* *This is building on the rock.*] The Author here anticipates the very good advice which all the *Reviewers* intend in future to give him ; that is, to build no more *Castles in the Air* ; but to return to his trade of building houses on the *rock*. And as those gentlemen are celebrated retailers of second-hand wit, he hopes they will be so very obliging as to favour him with that (by them at least) very much hackneyed adage,

Ne sutor ultra crepidam.

LOVE'S

LOVE'S ELOQUENCE.

A S O N G.

I.

OF T has my fault'ring tongue essay'd
   To paint my glowing heart,
Whilst vivid Fancy strove to aid,
   Warm Passion's honest art;
But language fails, all arts are vain,
   Tame reas'ning falls to nought;
Nor can the schoolmen's wit explain
   A lover's tender thought.

2.

Say, can yon pedant's lore express
   The language of the storms?

Or

Or in ftiff garb of fyftem drefs

  Wild Fancy's changing forms?

Attempts are vain, and vainer ftill,

  Effay the fons of Art;

They never can, with all their fkill,

  Tranflate the Lover's heart.

3.

The lips may Falfhood's form difguife,

  Whilft Innocence believes;

But Love and Truth have fpeaking eyes,

  Their language ne'er deceives;

Beware of him whofe wordy lay

  Thy weetlefs ear affails;

'Tis fell Deceit: O, turn away!

  Nor hear the Syren's tales.

4.

The timid air, the fhy advance,

  Th' involuntary tear;

                    The

The tender look, the wiftful glance,

   Are ever found fincere:

Then, Delia, read the wordlefs tale,

   By filence well exprefs'd ;

Mark what impaffion'd looks reveal

   The feelings of my breaft.

————————

B A N K s

BANKS OF THE DAW,

WRITTEN IN 1778.

DAW.—*The river that runs by the Author's native place.*

1.

OBEDIENT, sweet Mufe, to thy gentle command,
　　I lead, with warm feelings, thy numbers along;
O! bid thy bright flame in my bofom expand;
　　Bid all thy rich fancies replenifh my fong.
'Tis Nature all-charming this ardour infpires;
　　Carp on, my good Critics, I care not a ftraw;
I fing what no fquare-wielding Critic admires,
　　Wild beauty that fports on the *Banks of the Daw.*

2.

Here thickets romantic, irregular meads,

   In order fantaſtic ſeem ſcatter'd around;

'Tis Nature's gay plan, has a charm that exceeds

   All modes that in ſyſtem can ever be found;

This wild-winding river obſerve in the vale,

   'Tis Beauty's true line, which dull Art never ſaw,

By Fancy diſplay'd, where ſhe warbles her tale,

   To the raptnrous Bard on the *Banks of the Daw.*

3.

No vice-haunted cities encumber this plain;

   No glittering domes in falſe dignity ſwell;

The meek artleſs nymph, and her innocent ſwain,

   Here ſtill with mild Peace and Simplicity dwell;

'Tis the ſweet *Britiſh blackbird* that ſings in my grove;

   No *parrot* pedantic, no learned *macaw*;

And to hear my lov'd *nightingale* often I rove,

   Where the moon ſweetly ſilvers the *Banks of the Daw.*

4. On

4.

On the brow of yon hill a torn caſtle appears;

   Low humbled in rubbiſh old grandeur we trace;

The ruin yields now to the ravage of years,

   And Pomp's vain memorials all vaniſh apace.

Rough *Barons* are gone, and forgotten their fame,

   Who kept a rude race for long ages in awe:

But Nature, ſweet ruſtic, for ever the ſame,

   Still dwells with her Bard on the *Banks of the Daw*.

5.

No gaudy parterre here diſhonours the ground;

   No feats of dull Faſhion appear on theſe plains;

Here Beauty, dear charmer, wild wanders around,

   Unfetter'd by fools in Formality's chains:

No languiſhing ſhrub, a ſad exile, here mourns,

   Nipt in a ſtrange clime by the winter's keen flaw *;

* *Flaw.*] (Latin *flo*). A cold nipping gale, a ſudden blaſt.

      Vide Johnson's Dictionary, folio edition.

  O! that that earth that kept the world in awe,

  Should patch a wall t' expel the winter's flaw.

         Shakspeare.

But

But old *Britiſh* verdure luxuriant adorns

  The ſweet rural ſcene on the *Banks of the Daw*.

6.

Now May decks the meadows with beauty profuſe;

  The morning's rich odours repleniſh the gale;

'Tis the ſeaſon of ſong, and I'll woo the ſweet *Muſe*;

  She wanders where ſilence inhabits the dale:

The *Muſe*, for whoſe favours I treated with ſcorn

  The wealth that vile miſers rapaciouſly claw;

She, charmer of Nature, in Youth's early morn,

  I, liſping, invok'd on the *Banks of the Daw*.

7.

On the day (well remember'd) I dwell with delight,

  When in ſearch of her objects I wander'd afar;

To deep-ſounding ſhores, where the ſurge, in fierce

      might,

Aſſails the rude rock with perpetual war.

                      And

And often, whilſt Night ſoftly curtain'd the plain,

　　Would I from the village in ſilence withdraw ;

To paint my warm heart in young Paſſion's wild

　　　　　ſtrain,

　　And ſaunter alone on the *Banks of the Daw.*

8.

Enſlav'd by no paſſion, ſecluded from pride,

　　A ruſtic, inglorious, I dwell in this vale :

Let fools, lovely Nature, thy dictates deride,

　　I know thy ſweet voice, and attend to thy tale ;

And here may my moments glide peaceful along,

　　No conſcience upbraiding my boſom to gnaw ;

Thou, too, ſhall partake of thy Bard's humble ſong,

　　My dear native cot on the *Banks of the Daw.*

STOICISM.

S T O I C I S M.

1.

CANST thou the fangs of torture bear,
   To vulture knaves thy wealth refign,
      And dauntlefs drink thy cup of gall?
Say, canft thou quafh the ftruggling tear,
   Nor at thy woful fate repine,
      When foes triumphant fee thy fall?

2.

She, lovely darling of thy heart,
   Groans in the furious gripe of Death,
      Or venom'd foes revile her name;
Detraction, with infernal art,
   And green-ey'd Envy's blighting breath,
      Purfue thy merit's rifing fame.

3. If

3.

If ſtill unchang'd thy ſteady face,

   If no fierce feeling tears thy breaſt,

     If rend thy ſoul no ſuff'ring can ;

Thou art not ſprung of earthly race,

   Art of ſome nature ſtrange poſſeſs'd,

    Art, ſurely, *leſs* or *more* than MAN.

SONG.

S O N G.

1.

NOW day's chearful moments are fled,
  And each happy mortal asleep,
Whilst, quitting my slumberlefs bed,
  On the fea's rocky margent I weep;
By the foam-cover'd billow reclin'd,
  And fearching in vain for relief;
I utter my tale to the wind,
  My tale of unfpeakable grief.

2.

Amid the ftern horrors of night,
  Alone on the beach I complain;
My joys have all taken their flight;
  No fhadows of comfort remain

To the tide's hollow murmur I rave,

    Expending in fighs my fad breath;

My *Jemmy* lies under the wave,

    Lies deep in the manfions of death.

TO

TO THE CUCKOO,

WRITTEN IN 1775.

I.

HAIL! welcom'd Harbinger of Spring,
  Blithe Herald of the bloomy May;
The groves, the vales, harmonious ring,
  Refponfive to thy cheering lay;
And where the fwallow fkims along,
I ramble down the dale, and liften to thy fong.

2.

Thy voice recalls the fmiling hours;
  With thee returns the vernal morn;
And pearly dews, and fragrant flow'rs,
  Once more our verdant meads adorn,
When, through the vocal dells around,
The thrilling fongs of love in echo'd lays refound.

Vol. I.   D   3. Whilft

3.

Whilſt Winter quits thy fulgent ſkies,

 And Peace attends the roſy dawn,

Thy ſcenes employ my raptur'd eyes

 Where Beauty revels on the lawn;

With Joy's loud notes the welkin rings,

And Fancy mounts her throne, and waves her gol-

  den wings.

4.

Sweet Cuckoo, now thy morning mild

 Awakes to love the choral throng,

I range with thee the thicket wild,

 I tune with thee the rural ſong;

Here emulate thy cheerful voice,

Rouſe up my drooping Muſe, and bid my ſoul re-

  joice.

5.

Say, lovely gueſt! oh! wilt thou ſtay,

 Nor leave Britannia's favour'd iſle?

So shall the charms of youthful May

 Through ev'ry month serenely smile;

And Love, a monarch in thy train,

Shall rule in ev'ry soul, shall triumph on the plain.

6.

The mirthful Muse will daily chaunt

 The joys of thy delightful hour;

Thy song will bless the Lover's haunt,

 Thy sylvan Bard's secluded bow'r;

Stay, sweet enliv'ner of the dale,

And wake up ev'ry dawn with thy rejoicing tale.

7.

Alas! ere long thy soothing note

 No more shall cheer the pallid morn;

Nor tow'ring lark in ether float;

 Nor blackbird warble on the thorn:

Stern Winter meets our sadden'd eyes;

Amid the storm enthron'd, the tyrant of the skies.

8. Fond

8.

Fond youth attend, the leſſon 's thine!

   So fleet apace thy mirthful hours;

Life's jocund ſpring will ſoon decline;

   Thy joys will fade like drooping flow'rs;

Time leaves behind thy tuneful days,

And Age with icy cares will ſtrew thy wintry ways.

9.

May ſhall frequent the groves again,

   The Cuckoo ſing on ev'ry tree,

Bright Beauty's mantle robe the plain,

   But Spring returns no more for thee:

Where art thou gone? ah! whither fled?

Forgotten in the grave, low number'd with the dead.

10.

Liv'd conſcious Goodneſs in thy breaſt?

   Dwelt Truth an inmate of thy heart?

Was Virtue by thy ſoul careſs'd,

   When Death bade fly th' unerring dart?

                       Then

Then wing'd thy raptur'd foul away,
To thofe eternal climes where ev'ry month is May.

This piece was printed in the Town and Country Magazine, for July, 1775. It is here confiderably altered; but the fentiments are ftill the fame, and in the fame arrangement. A piece on the fame fubject appeared in a fmall volume of Poems that was pub-lifhed about feven or eight years after; where the fimilarity appears fo ftriking, that one of thefe Poems cannot well be confidered but as a ftudied imitation of the other; how far this can be fuppofed to be incidental, muft be left to the public opinion.

ADVICE TO A WHINING LOVER.

1.

WAND'RER of the pathlefs plain,
  Why that fob of filly care?
Hugging ftill thy galling chain;
  Whining to the midnight air.

2.

Why, with owls amid the grove,
  Wilt thou fhun the cheerful day?
And, in doleful fongs of love,
  Sadly fool thy life away.

3.

Thee, through brakes and boggy meads,
  Pelted by the ftorms of night,
Love, a jack-a-lanthorn, leads,
  Gleaming with perfidious light.

4. Thee,

4.

Thee, deprefs'd by dire alarms,
　　Moping near the fedgy brook
Have I feen, with folded arms,
　　Love-fick phiz, and fheepifh look.

5.

Phœbe flights thy proffer'd love;
　　Phœbe triumphs in thy pain;
Nought can Phœbe's pity move;
　　Nought affuage her high difdain.

6.

Haplefs doom! and why wilt thou
　　Still her fetter'd flave remain?
Here's the rope, and there's the bough,
　　Certain cures for all thy pain.

7.

Hafte! thy crufhing load of grief
　　On yon blafted oak fufpend;
'Tis the lover's beft relief;
　　This will foon thy forrows end.

'D 4　　　　　　8. Then,

8.

Then, from Phœbe's bondage free,

    To that wench no more a flave ;

Thou fhalt triumph on the tree,

    Like a lover bold and brave.

9.

Then, a ghoft of fainted fame,

    When around the ravens fly,

Thou fhalt fing with loud acclaim,

    " Love has won the victory."

10.

And thy form will furely pleafe,

    When her martyr Phœbe finds,

Dangling with a graceful eafe,

    Devious in the ftormy winds.

11.

Thus, exalted to the fkies,

    Thou fhalt thrilling joys impart

To thy Phœbe's ravifh'd eyes ;

    To thy charmer's tender heart.

12. Gloomy

12.

Gloomy Lovers in defpair

   Shall for ever crowd thy fhrine;

Sigh to thee their fniv'ling care;

   Raife to thee the wonted whine.

13.

Phœbe, with exulting boaft,

   Shall proclaim her Damon true;

This will charm thy raptur'd ghoft;

   Hafte! and bid the world adieu!

———————

THE

THE REAPERS.

A PASTORAL.

(Inscribed to the GLAMORGAN *Agricultural Society.)*

I.

ALL up with the Sun, the brisk reapers were
    seen,
Prepar'd with their sickles, and walking the green;
The lads whistle jocund, their lasses attend
At Love's tender call, sweet assistance to lend;
As gamesome along, through the morning's fresh
    air,
The gay village-throng to the wheat-field repair,
Blithe *Corydon*, tuning his musical tongue,
Thus the praises of rural felicity sung.

                     2. CORYDON,

2.

CORYDON.

The carol of gladnefs is due to this day,

Ye lads and ye laffes attend to my lay.

Ye that from high Pride's bloating paffions are free,

And join in the labours of harveft with me,

I fing of your honours, I fing of your wealth,

Your days of contentment, your bleffings of health ;

The virtues, the joys, of thofe peaceable fwains,

Who, pupils of Nature, inhabit the plains.

3.

Let thofe that abide in the filth of a town

Deride, if they pleafe, the meek life of a clown ;

We laugh at their tinfel, our tafte is too nice

To be pleas'd with their toys, or to relifh their vice ;

In worthlefs purfuits let them fquander their time,

Their luxuries love, and fall off in their prime ;

Whilft we, rural fwains, in low villages find

Rich plenty, fweet health, and a peaceable mind.

4. How

4.

How happy the life of an innocent fwain,

'That dwells with his herds and his flocks on the

    plain ;

Who labours abroad on his farm all the day,

Now turning his fallows, now tedding his hay ;

Here cattle in fields of rich clover we view ;

Here lambkins in meads of a beautiful hue ;

And here the rich fruits of his labours we find,

Where the wheat's golden curls * gently wave in the

    wind.

5.

He flights the pretenfions of Grandeur and Wealth,

And thinks them furpafs'd by Contentment and

    Health ;

---

* Golden curls.] Now the Author dares venture his life that there is not a Paftoral wr ter in all Grub-ftreet that knows any thing of the wheat's golden curls.——Poor Devils !

His.

His well-founded hopes are by Providence blefs'd,

And on it's protection with coi fidence reft :

He whiftles and fings as he rambles his farm,

Loves innocent mirth, and he thinks it no harm ;

By blifsful experience, he feelingly knows

The folid content that from induftry flows.

6.

'Tis Induftry's toil ev'ry comfort fecures,

The fweeteft enjoyments of Nature infures ;

Warm raiment, fweet food, from its hand we de-
rive ;

It fofters, and keeps all the virtues alive ;

It planted the rofe that yon garden adorns,

Where grew the rank hemlock with venomous
thorns ;

It gives ev'ry feeling a polifh refin'd,

And calms the rude paffions, and brightens the mind.

7.

When cold furly ftorms of bleak Winter appear,

The fwain that 's induftrious has nothing to fear;

Though

Though round him proud hills are all cover'd with
      snow,

Though streams are congeal'd in the vallies below,

With plenty well-suiting his humble desire,

He cheerfully sits by the side of his fire;

His moments of peace leading jocund along,

With stories of old, or a merry new song.

8.

The skies are now bright, we repair to the field,

Nor lags one behind that a sickle can wield;

The hills and the vales shall resound with our din;

We 'll joyfully bustle till harvest is in;

Or if for a moment to rest we sit down,

We 'll merrily jeer the fine folk of the town,

Who trifle their lives in dull follies away,

And see the Sun shine, but neglect to make hay.

9.

Thus *Corydon* sang to glad hearers around,

Loud shouts of applause bade the welkin resound;

                               We

We now the ripe corn widely falling behold,

So fell before Arthur the *Saxons* of old :

Anon the good farmer's neat maidens appear,

They toil under loads of *old British* good cheer ;

The laffes are kifs'd, then the reapers regale,

And the fong comes again o'er a cup of good ale.

LOVE

LOVE   TRIUMPHANT.

A   SONG.

1.

D A M O N, a flave in Celia's chain,

Had various efforts tried in vain

    To win the cruel maid ;

Now, penfive in the tangled grove,

He, ftruggling in the toils of Love,

    Calls Reafon to his aid.

2.

" Come, god-like Reafon ! and impart

" Thy nob'er motives to my heart ;

    " O ! calm this troubled breaft :

                   " Dif-

" Difpel mad Paffion's vain alarms,

" And let, once more, thy brighter charms

" Reftore my foul to reft.

3.

" Blind Love! thou fource of endlefs pain,

" Thou dream in Fancy's giddy brain,

" Whilft carelefs Reafon fleeps :

" Caught in thy fnare, man's high-born mind

" Debas'd, amongft the reptile kind,

" Through Folly's puddle creeps.

4.

" I foar! I feel my foul unchain'd!

" My former liberty regain'd!

" And Celia 's nought to me !

" Now, Reafon! I'm for ever thine!

" I all my future days refign

" To Friendfhip and to thee!

5. " No.

5.

" No more the dupe of female art,

" I tear thee, Celia, from my heart !

   " This heart once more my own !

" Thy charms are vanifh'd all away !

" Thus, from the golden blaze of day,

   " The fhades of night are flown."

6.

Affronted thus, almighty Love

Drew Celia to the darkling grove,

   Near Damon's lone retreat !

Again the ranter proftrate lay,

His boafted *Reafon* breath'd away

   In fighs, at Celia's feet !

WRITTEN

WRITTEN AT THE CLOSE OF AUTUMN,

1778.

1.

WHEN youthful Spring, in flow'ry mantle gay,
Led on the jocund hours of smiling May,
 My Muse attun'd the joy-proclaiming song,
With aged Autumn, penfive o'er the plain,
Attempt I now the fentimental ftrain,
 By fofter feelings mov'd, the fadden'd fcene along.

2.

No cheerful fongfter ufliers in the dawn,
No gorgeous bloom enrobes the joylefs lawn,
 No nightingale awakes the midnight hour ;
Yet fading Nature gives the tender mind
A mournful blifs, a feeling more refin'd,
 Than aught wild Mirth enjoys in May's em-
  bloffom'd bow'r.

3. Th'

3.

Th' obfervant Bard, a devious Hermit, roves

To vales remote, and far-fequefter'd groves,

 Or where wild furges lafh the founding fhore;

Whilft from the mountains ruder gales arife,

He, wiftful, notes the ftorm-foreboding fkies;

 Or hears (and drops a tear) the diftant cannon.

  roar.

4.

Fond of the moral drawn from Nature's lore,

He marks the falling leaf, the landfcape hoar,

 And ruminates on all the boaft of youth;

How Summer's pride to rifling Winter yields,

How Beauty fpeaks, expiring on the fields,

 To man's unheeding ear. th' emphatic word of

  Truth.

5.

Here Morning triumph'd, bright in pearly dews,

Here bloom'd the lawn in May's unrival'd hues,

 Here vocal groves with Love's gay carols rung;

       The

'The lawn's high bloom, the morn in mantle bright,

Are loft; all vanifh'd from the mournful fight;

    And hufh'd the fylvan founds of Joy's extatic

        tongue:

6.

Ye flaunting Beauties, who thro' blooming youth,

Seldom attend the cherub voice of Truth,

    By Flatt'ry deafen'd, and by Folly led;

Behold where once the gaudy tulip bloom'd!

Where once the pink its ambient air perfum'd!

    Where proud the lily once high rear'd its gor-

        geous head!

7.

Alas! their charms are vanifh'd all away,

They glare no more in the bright blaze of day,

    Nor fruit nectareous leave in Beauty's room;

The wither'd ftem, expos'd to raging ftorms,

Alone remains, and Nature's face deforms,

    In Winter's frowning morn augments the dreary

        gloom.

8. Ye

8.

Ye Fair attend! nor truſt the blooming face;

Youth quickly flies, and beauty fades apace,

    It hardly knows the triumph of a day;

'Tis Virtue's glow beſtows unfading charms,

Its bloom divine the ſoul of Reaſon warms,

    Nor thro' duration's round e'er feels the leaſt

    decay.

9.

Behold yon apple tree with tow'ring height,

Undaunted brave the ſtorm's collected ſpite,

    May view'd it rob'd in Beauty's bloomy veſt;

Each loaded branch, with fruit ambroſial grac'd,

Now glads the ſight, now charms th' extatic taſte;

    Chief of ſurrounding woods in real worth con-

    feſs'd.

10.

Thus, Della, thy ſweet innocence of youth

Produc'd the fair, the ripen'd, fruits of Truth,

    Of 'dove-eyed Goodneſs, and a taſte refin'd,

By

By Reafon cultur'd in thy feeling heart,

The growth abundant fprings in ev'ry part;

 And Truth's eternal bloom enrobes thy beau-

 teous mind.

11.

Come, lovely Maid, and with thy thoughtful fwain,

View Nature drooping on the wither'd plain;

 Bleak Winter foon will ev'ry fcene deform;

Will bid its rage through ruftling thickets fly,

Bid chilly fnows on Earth's cold bofom lie;

 Chain up the purling brook, and urge along the

 ftorm.

12.

Yet fhall the joyful Spring again return,

And bid reviving Nature ceafe to mourn,

 May's bloom awaken from the teeming earth;

See, Delia, fee, this picture of that day,

When the rapt foul breaks through this cage of clay,

 Springs up to life again in a celeftial birth.

13. Though

13.

Though Grief and Pain may cloud our wintry day,

Whilst thro' this life, this defart bleak, we ftray,

    Yet Hope attends us, hand in hand with Peace;

Sweet Hope! that healer of the bleeding breaft,

Leads her meek vot'ries to the calm of reft,

    Smiles in the humble heart, and bids all forrow

    ceafe.

14.

Why fear we Death? why wifh its long delay?

Death kindly bears us to thofe realms of day,

    Whence Anguifh flies, and ne'er returns again:

Calm Reafon fmiles, and hails the blifsful hour,

That frees the foul from erring Frailty's pow'r,

    From all her earth-born ills of Folly, Grief,

    and Pain.

15.

Let balmy Hope antisipate the joy

That fhall eternally our thoughts employ,

    When, in thofe manfions of the blefs'd above,

                                           We

We meet our friends, releas'd from death and pain,

One common Friend unites us all again,

 Whofe fmile is endlefs Peace, and everlafting

 Love.

THE FAIR PILGRIM;

From Dafydd ap Gwilym, a Welſh Bard, who flouriſhed about the Year 1350.

THE Charmer of ſweet MONA's * Iſle,
With Death attendant on her ſmile,
Intent on pilgrimage divine,
Speeds to Saint DAVID's † holy ſhrine;
Too conſcious of a ſinful mind,
And hopes ſhe may forgiveneſs find.

  What haſt thou done, thrice lovely maid ?
What crimes can to thy charge be laid ?

---

* MONA,] the Iſle of *Angleſea*.

† St. DAVID] was, in thoſe times, reckoned the tutelary Saint of Wales.

                                        Didſt

Didſt thou contemn the ſuppliant Poor,

Drive helpleſs Orphans from thy door,

Unduteous to thy parents prove,

Or yield thy charms to lawleſs Love?

No, MORVID, no; thy gentle breaſt

Was form'd to pity the Diſtreſs'd;

Has ne'er one thought, one feeling known,

That Virtue could not call her own;

Nor haſt thou caus'd a parent's pain

Till quitting now thy native plain.

Yet, lovely nymph, thy way purſue,

And keep repentance full in view;

Yield not thy tongue to cold reſtraint,

But lay thy ſoul before the Saint;

Oh! tell him that thy lover dies;

On Death's cold bed unpitied lies;

Murder'd by thee, relentleſs maid,

And to th' untimely grave convey'd.

Yet ere he 's number'd with the dead,

Ere yet his lateſt breath is fled;

Con-

Confefs, repent, thou cruel Fair,

And hear, for once, a Lover's pray'r,

So may the Saint with ear benign,

Sweet Penitent, attend to thine.

    Thou foon muft over MENAI * go;

May ev'ry current foftly flow,

Thy little bark fecurely glide

Swift o'er the calm pellucid tide;

Unruffled be thy gentle breaft,

Without one fear to break thy reft,

Till thou art fafely wafted o'er,

To bold ARVONIA's † tow'ring fhore.

    O! could I guard thy lovely form

Safe through yon defart of the ftorm ‡,

---

  * MENAI,] the frith or channel dividing *Anglefea* from *Car-*
narvonfhire.

   † ARVONIA,] *Carnarvonfhire.*

   ‡ *Defart of the ftorm,*] the *Snowdon Mountains* in Carnarvon-
fhire, fuppofed to be the higheft in *Britain.*

Where

Where fiercely rage encount'ring gales,

And whirlwinds rend th' affrighted vales;

Sons of the tempeft, ceafe to blow,

Sleep in your cavern'd glens below;

Ye ftreams that, with terrific found,

Pour from your thoufand hills around;

Ceafe with rude clamours to difmay

A gentle Pilgrim on her way.

　　Peace! rude TRAETH MAWR *; no longer urge

O'er thy wild ftrand the fweeping furge;

'Tis MORVID on thy beach appears,

She dreads thy wrath—fhe owns her fears;

O! let the meek repentant maid

Securely through thy windings wade.

---

* TRAETH MAWR] (*Anglicè*, *Great Strand*), in *Carnarvon-fhire*, noted for its quickfands, and the fudden flowing of its tides; the paffage over it is very dangerous, and not to be attempted without a guide, which, however, the Pilgrims to St. DAVID's did in thofe days.

TRAETH BYCHAN *, check thy dreadful ire;

And bid thy foamy waves retire;

Till from thy threat'ning dangers freed,

My charmer trips the flow'ry mead,

Then bid again with fullen roar,

Thy billows lafh the founding fhore.

ABERMO †, from thy rocky bay,

Drive each terriffic furge away :

Though funk beneath thy billows lie

Proud fanes, that once affail'd the fky ‡.

Dafh'd

---

* TRAETH BYCHAN] (*Little Strand*), in *Merionethfhire*, a place equally dangerous.

† ABERMO,] a dangerous rocky bay in *Merionethfhire*.

‡ *Proud fanes that once affail'd the fky.*] A very large tract of fenny country on this coaft, called CANTRE'R GWAELOD (i. e. the LOWLAND CANTON), was, about the year 500, overflown by the fea, occafioned by the carelefsnefs of thofe who kept the flood-gates; as we are informed by *Taliefin,* the famous Bard, in a poem of his ftill extant. There were, it is faid, many large towns, a great number of villages, and palaces of noble-
men,

Dafh'd by thy foam, yon veftal braves,

The dangers of thy burfting waves.

O! Cyric *, fee my lovely fair

Confign'd to thy paternal care;

Rebuke the raging feas, and land

My Morvid on yon friendly ftrand.

Dyssynni †, tame thy furious tide,

Fix'd at thy fource in peace abide ;

She comes—O! greet her with a fmile !—

The charmer of fweet Mona's Ifle.

So may thy limpid rills around,

Purl down their dells with foothing found,

men, in this canton; and amongft them the palace of Gwydd-no Garanhir, a petty Prince of the country. There were lately (and I believe are ftill) to be feen in the fands of this bay, large ftones with infcriptions on them, the characters Roman, but the language unknown.—This difaftrous circumftance is re-corded by many other ancient Welfh Writers.

* Cyric.] The patron Saint of the Welfh mariners.

† Dyssynni.] A river in *Merionethfhire*, running through a beautiful country.

Sport on thy bofom, and difplay

Their cryftal to the glitt'ring day;

Nor fhrink from Summer's parching fun,

Nor, chain'd in ice, forget to run.

So may thy verdant marge along

MERVINIA's * Bards in raptur'd fong:

Dwell on thy bold majeftic fcene,

Huge hills, vaft woods, and vallies green,

Where revels thy enchanting ftream,

The Lover's haunt, and Poet's theme.

Thou, DYVI †, dangerous and deep,

On beds of ooze unruffled fleep;

O'er thy green wave my MORVID ‡ fails;

Conduct her fafe, ye gentle gales;

Charm'd

---

* MERVINIA.] *Merionethfbire.*

† DYVI.] A large-river, dividing *Merionethfbire* from *Cardiganfbire.*

‡ *My* MORVID *fails.*] It was ufual for thofe (even females), who went from North Wales on pilgrimages to St. DAVID's, to pafs the dangerous ftrands, and fail over the rough bays, in

flight

Charm'd with her beauties, waft her o'er

To fain'd CEREDIG's * wond'ring fhore.

Foamy RHEDIOL †, rage no more

Down thy rocks with echo'd roar;

Be filent, YSTWYTH †, in thy meads,

Glide foftly through thy peaceful reeds;

Nor bid thy dells rude AERON † ring,

But halt at thy maternal fpring;

Hide from the nymph, ye torrents wild,

Or wear, like her, an afpect mild;

For her light fteps clear all your ways;

O, liften! 'tis a Lover prays!

flight coracles, without any one to guide or affift them; fo firmly were they perfuaded that their adored Saint, as well as CYRIC, the ruler of the waves, would protect them in all dangers. See the note in p. 77.

* CEREDIG.] An ancient Prince, from whom *Ceredigion* (*Anglicè, Cardigan*) derives its name.

† RHEDIOL, YSTWYTH, and AERON, rivers in *Cardiganfhire*.

Now fafe beneath ferener fkies,

Where fofter beauties charm her eyes,

She TEIVI's * verdant region roves,

Views flow'ry meads and penfile groves;

Ye lovely fcenes, to MORVID's heart,

Warm thoughts of tendernefs impart,

Such as in bufy tumults roll,

When Love's confufion fills the foul.

Her wearied ftep, with awe profound,

Now treads MENEVIA's † honour'd ground.

At

---

* TEIVI.] A large river dividing the counties of *Cardigan*
and *Pembroke.*

† MENEVIA.] In Welfh *Mynyw*, the ancient city of *St.
David's*, in *Pembrokefhire.* The pilgrimages to this place were,
in thofe times, efteemed fo very meritorious, as to occafion the
following proverbial rhyme in Welfh :

   Dôs i Rufain unwaith, ag i Fynyw ddwywaith,
   A'r un elw cryno a gai di yma ac yno.

And in Latin :
   Roma *femel quantum, bis dat* Menevia *tantum.*

Would

At DAVID's fhrine now, lovely maid,

Thy pious orifons are paid:

He fees the fecrets of thy breaft,

One fin, one only ftands confefs'd,

One heinous guilt, that, ruthlefs, gave

Thy hopelefs Lover to the grave.

Thy foften'd bofom now relents,

Of all its cruelty repents,

Would haughty *Popes* your fenfes bubble,
    And once to *Rome* your fteps entice ;
'Tis quite as well, and faves fome trouble,
    Go vifit old Saint *Taffy* twice.

The Welfh Bard's moft refpectful compliments to their *infal-libl* Holineffes the POPES of all fects and denominations (for fuch there certainly are), and hopes they will pardon him for not giving a clofer verfion of the good old *Monk's* jingling line ; affures them that he has not taken greater liberties with it than what they daily take with the *Bible* (and indeed with all *txub* in general), well-knowing that it will not fully anfwer their *laudable* purpofes without a little *decent* perverfion.

         Gives

Gives to Remorfe the fervent figh,

Sweet Pity's tear bedews thine eye ;

Now Love lights up its hallow'd fire,

Melts all thy heart with chafte defire :

Whilft in thy foul new feelings burn,

O ! Morvid, to thy Bard return ;

One tender look will cure his pain,

Will bid him rife to life again,

A life like that of Saints above,

Extatic joy, and endlefs love.

———————

THE

THE LEARNED IGNORANTS,

A   S O N G,

WRITTEN IN 1772.

1.

YE book-poring pedants, by learning made fools,

Whofe fkulls are well-ftuff'd with the rubbifh of

fchools,

Ye boaft your old *ballads* that claffics ye call,

Your *Homers*, your *Virgils*, your devil and all;

True, ye know *Greek* enough to make any dog fick,

Nor lefs are ye fkill'd in the cant of *Old Nick*;

But, how does it happen? ye conftantly prove

Mere dunces indeed in the language of *Love.*

2.

A tatter'd *Oxonian* I t' other day met,

One of thofe that make books (I was quite in a pet),

He was filching from *Horace* old thoughts for a fong,

Where through the green wood I walk'd penfive

    along ;

He look'd wild around him, and afk'd with fur-

    prize,

If Duns or Bumbailiffs occafion'd my fighs,

But I fought my dear Phillis, and flew from the grove,

Alas ! the poor *Soph* knows but little of *Love*.

3.

Once forc'd from my charmer abruptly to part,

Grief harrow'd my foul, drew the blood from my

    heart ;

In my way an abfurd aftronomical afs

Bo-peep'd at the fky through a queer-fafhion'd glafs ;

He faw my fad looks, and the briny tears run,

And fuppos'd 'twas by ftaring, like him, at the

    Sun ;

At the Sun! yes, you block-head, but not that above,

'Twas a brighter by far, the bright eyes of my *Love.*

4.

One morning in May, as I walk'd by the rill

That tinkles along near the foot of yon hill,

Gay Spring bloom'd around, how ſerene the ſweet

    air,

And, weeping, I wiſh'd my dear *Phillis* was there;

When a booby old *Botaniſt*, haunting the place,

Through a pair of broad ſpectacles ſtar'd in my face;

This *eye-ſeed*, quoth he, will your anguiſh remove :—

'Twas a *weed-monger's* tale, that knew nothing of

    Love.

5.

As ſaunt'ring laſt night in the pine-ſhaded walk,

Where often I'm bleſs'd with my charmer's dear

    talk ;

I long'd to behold her, look'd anxious around,

But my fair-one, alas! was no where to be found ;

                  A

A *Philosopher* ask'd, if I wept, sigh'd, and whin'd,
Like *Heraclitus* once, for the whims of mankind?
A *Philosopher* you! that's amazing, by Jove!
And ignorant thus of the nature of *Love*.

6.

In a glade far-sequester'd, as lately retir'd,
I wept the sad absence of her I admir'd;
When a son of old *Galen* came hobbling that way,
And, like other dull sots, wanted something to say;
He ask'd me, observing my tears and my sighs,
If a *lachrymal fistula* flooded my eyes?
Alas, the poor *Doctor!* 'twas easy to prove
His heart never felt the keen *lancet* of *Love*.

7.

As, weeping, I pass'd by the church t' other day,
In search of my Phillis who rambled that way;
I was taken to task by a preaching old *prig*,
'Twas a *double-chinn'd Priest*, in a full-bottom'd wig;
He of fasting and pray'r made a wonderful din,
And hop'd, he pretended, I wept for my sin;

But

But how can *be* claim thofe blefs'd manfions above,

That's not of the faith and religion of *Love?*,

8.

The billet from Phillis, her hand and her feal,

Drew me out of the parlour my tears to conceal;

When a grizzly old *Alchymift* meets me, and cries,

" You 've been toiling in fmoke, I perceive by your

    " eyes;"

His *Philofopher's ftone* turns a brick-bat to gold,

Yet *Love's* nobler effence he ne'er could unfold;

But I flew to my charmer, we met in the grove,

And join'd foul to foul in th' endearments of *Love.*

9.

Hufh, Pedants, be mute! you may think me quite

    rude,

Becaufe I dare thus on your ftudies intrude;

But quit this dull farce, your poor college gri-

    mace,

And ftudy the charms of a *pretty girl's* face;

                    The

The tender expreffions of love-tutor'd eyes;

And conftrue the language of heart-fpeaking fighs;

Do this, and your learning to wifdom improve,

And you 'll own that true knowledge is nothing but

    Love !

————————

SADNESS.

S A D N E S S.

H O W sad the meek Innocent harrass'd by Spite,

Sad mourns the poor Pilgrim o'ertaken by Night;

And sadly droops Merit when Envy pursues ;

Good Nature too saddens if cross'd in her views.

Disease and keen Want will make ev'ry one sad ;

The loss of sweet Liberty 's equally bad.

Sad weighs the long debt on each honest man's
    heart ;

But saddest of *all*, that true Lovers must part.

—————————————

T H E

THE SWAIN OF THE MOUNTAINS,

A PASTORAL,

In the Welſh Manner.

I.

WHEN ſmiling Felicity warbles her ſong,
  The ſoul-touching numbers harmoniouy flow ,
The moments of Gladneſs come urgent along,
  And bid all the feelings of ecſtacy glow.
Thus, reclin'd with his lambs on the marge of a
    brook,
  The Swain of the Mountains melodiouſly ſung ;
The ſun-ſhine of Happineſs beam'd in his look ;
  Joy trill'd in the ſound of his muſical tongue.

2. Far

2.

Far down in this dale, the first morning in June,

    I mournfully walk'd near the murmuring rill,

The Thrush in wild melody warbled his tune,

    From a gay-blooming bush of the copse-cover'd
       hill.

Sweet Thrush, wilt thou leave thy green haunts in
       the grove,

    And fly, quickly fly, with my dolorous tale

To the pride of the Lowlands, the fair one I love ?

    I 'll wait thy return here alone in the vale.

3.

Now to the wild woodlands I fly from the mead,

    And through the lone thicket I silently mourn ;

Go, Thrush, haste away with a Lover's warm speed,

    Beneath thy lov'd hawthorn I wait thy return:

Now pensively rambling, now laid on the ground,

    I strive to beguile the sad moments of grief;

I search the green copse and gay meadows around,

    But nothing, alas ! can afford me relief.

4. The

4.

The thicket's wild fongfter flew fwift o'er the plain,

 Convey'd to my Delia the paffionate lay ;

My anguifh related, well-pictur'd my pain,

 And bore three foft fighs from my charmer away.

Returning in hafte, yonder comes my fweet Thrufh :

 Approach thy green arbour, no danger lies here ;

What haft thou to chaunt on thy favourite bufh ?

 What tidings of comfort ? what news from my

  dear ?

5.

I flew to thy Delia, fhe faunter'd alone,

 On her eglantine bow'r I related thy tale,

Thy forrowful ditty, thy mufical moan,

 Attun'd her to love,—all thy wifhes prevail ;

Be cheer'd, penfive fhepherd, no longer delay,

 Thefe fighs are thy Delia's, they rufh'd on the

  gale ;

On pinions of Love to thy fair hafte away,

 This ev'ning fhe 'll meet thee far down in the dale.

6.

I flew to my nymph on the wings of defire,

  In her eglantine bow'r fhe fat penfive and fad ;

I kifs'd her dear lips, and Love's delicate fire

  Blaz'd up in our hearts, both were filently glad.

Sweet Thrufh of the copfe, chaunt again thy wild tune,

  And let my blefs'd fate through the vallies be

    known ;

My Delia comply'd the third morning in June,

  The Swain of the Mountains now calls her his own.

———

In this piece many of the peculiarities of the common fongs of Wales are defignedly introduced, as a
fpecimen of the old national manner of the Welfh
in their Poems, and particularly in their *Love-fongs.*
Strong metaphors, wild and fudden tranfitions,
ftrange, and fometimes fantaftical, perfonifications,
are amongft the characteriftics of the Poetry of ancient and modern Welfh Bards. It is rather remark-
able,

able, that this nationality in poetic tafte fhould ftill be retained unaltered, when at the fame time the inhabitants of Wales are not much, if any thing, behind other European nations in their acquaintance with ancient and modern literature.

———————

HYMN

HYMN TO HEALTH,

WRITTEN IN MAY 1780,

On Recovery from a long and dangerous Illnefs.

Now tuneful on the bloomy thorn
The mellow blackbird hails the morn,
With placid gleam the purple dawn
Unveils the beauties of the lawn,
Through dewy dales and waving groves,
The vernal breeze unruffled roves.

　Delicious Health! I range the vale,
And breathe once more thy balmy gale;
'Scap'd from the wrathful fangs of pain,
I view, rejoic'd, thy fkies again;

Vol. I.　　　　F　　　　O, Sun!

O, Sun ! with raptur'd look I fee,

Thy fulgence beam again for me ;

　Thee to thefe eyes a ftranger long,

I hail once more in joyful fong ;

Once more I trace the fylvan fcene

Of daified field, and thicket green ;

In lays of grateful ardour fing,

And join the chorifters of Spring ;

Feel tranfport thrill in ev'ry vein,

Aftonifh'd that I breathe again.

　What is the boaft of titled *Wealth* ?

What, without thee, foul-cheering *Health* ?

Spring decks in vain her flow'ry lawn,

In vain her larks roufe up the dawn ;

Though, proud of Beauty's rich excefs,

Gay *Summer* wears her gorgeous drefs,

Or *Autumn* in profufion pours

Her golden wealth, her honied ftores ;

Thefe yield no joy, revolve in vain,

To that fad bofom rent with pain.

Gay

Gay *Fancy* feels a deadly froſt;

Bright *Reaſon's* energies are loſt;

Love's rapture dies, it's warm delight

Flies woful from the ſicken'd fight;

The *Muſe*, from all her pleaſures torn,

Her ſtrain forgets, and droops forlorn;

Affection brings her tear of grief,

But weeping friends yield no relief,

Where vanquiſh'd *Patience* vents her breath

In woful fighs that call for Death.

What *Angel* fings with heav'nly voice?

What bids my wond'ring heart rejoice?

Entrancing *Health!* 'tis thy return;

My plaints are huſh'd, I ceaſe to mourn;

Joy blooms around, thy ſmiles impart

Extatic feelings to my heart;

Of eaſe, of comfort, re-poſſeſs'd,

What thrills of gladneſs fill my breaſt!

I muſe impaſſion'd on thy charms,

And court thee wiſtful to my arms;

Obey

Obey thy laws, and trace for thee

The paths of cool *Sobriety*,

From cates of *luxury* refrain ;

No midnight bowl inflames my brain ;

My garden stores, my streamlet nigh,

Can well thy sanction'd board supply ;

Immers'd in cryftal waves I feek

The blooming rofes of thy cheek ;

I daily meet thy golden dawn,

Imbibe thy breezes on the lawn,

Climb rugged fteeps, and often tread

Yon funny mountain's ancient head,

What time the lark forfakes the plain,

To mount the fkies in merry vein ;

What time the milk-maid in the vale ·

Sings tuneful as the nightingale ;

And hears her lays in echo'd fwell,

Re-warbled through the vocal dell.

Doft thou prefcribe the toiling hand ?

I will obey thy blefs'd command ;

And,

And, where yon prickly thiftle grows,

Will rear the peach, and plant the rofe ;

Or feed my flocks, a fylvan fwain,

Inglorious on the peaceful plain ;

Will rife before th' autumnal Sun,

To range the fields with dog and gun ;

Attentive watch the peep of morn,

To chace the fox with hound and horn ;

In mirthful innocence refort

To manly feats of rural fport :

With nerve elaftic, ftrength renew'd,

And all thy foes, bright Health, fubdu'd,

The purple flood fhall ftream alert

Through all the channels of my heart ;

Through ev'ry limb untainted roll,

And give new vigours to the foul.

When comes Dejeftion's feeble thought,

With liftlefs Melancholy fraught,

I quit fad mufings, and attend

The focial converfe of a friend ;

Bid

Bid watchful Reafon chace the peft

Of fancy'd evils from my breaft;

The cheerful Mufe, with foothing art,

Shall purge the venom from my heart;

O, *Health!* her fervid feelings burn

To celebrate thy blefs'd return;

Sweet is her taſk in raptur'd lay

To fing of anguiſh flown away;

To Heav'n's high gates, in grateful fong,

She rolls her gladden'd thoughts along;

Bids her felected numbers rife,

With Joy's redundance, to the ſkies,

To Him who ſtay'd my parting breath,

Who drew me from the gorge of Death;

Who quench'd the fcorching flame of Pain,

And long-loſt Health reftor'd again;

Whofe goodnefs heard my groan of Grief:

Whofe hand of Mercy brought relief.

INSCRIPTION IN A GROTTO,

TO THE MEMORY OF THE LATE

E A R L   O F   C H A T H A M.

IN emulative ſtrains let others tell

What Britain loſt, when her Great CHATHAM fell!

Here Grief unfeign'd, to Flatt'ry ne'er a ſlave,

Retires to weep in this ſequeſter'd cave:

And, whilſt his glories fill the trump of Fame,

On this *eternal rock* inſcribes his NAME.

F 4   O N

ON RELIGION;

AN EPISTLE TO A FRIEND,

Who had expreſſed a Wiſh to know the Author's

Sentiments on the Subject ;

WRITTEN IN 1779.

" *Slave to no Party, Bigot to no Sect.*"   ANON.

I.

YOU aſk, my dear friend, what Religion I chuſe,
 What modes of belief I profeſs ;
For wanting Religion, I grant it, the Muſe
 Is depriv'd of her beautiful dreſs.

      2. 'Tis

2.

'Tis not that Religion impos'd on mankind

By *Popes,* crafty *Knaves,* and *Old Nick*;

A fpurious Religion, that darkens the mind;

That cankers the foul to the quick.

3.

The Mufe that from Heaven derives her high birth,

Recalls her employments above;

Believing, whilft here a poor pilgrim on Earth,

The *Gofpel* Religion of *Love.*

4.

No *creeds* can this *priefflefs* Religion define,

It baffles all *human* controul;

But dwells in the *Confcience,* a fervor divine,

To *blefs* and *illumine* the foul.

5.

By the Great *Prince of Peace,* 'tis meek Charity nam'd;

I ftrive its bright beauties to fcan;

'Tis *Glory to God,* and, as *Angels* proclaim'd,

'Tis *Peace and Good-will towards Man.*

F 5   Far

6.

Far spreads the Religion of *Av'rice* and *Pride*,
    From the *Tyrant's* high rostrum it rings ;
'Tis *Priestcraft in grain*, its dominions are wide,
    Well-castled by *Bishops* and *Kings*.

7.

Where find we the realm where *Christianity* rules ?
    Where it's code of *Benevolence* binds ?
The doctrines of *Love* are made, sadly, the tools
    Of selfish malevolent minds.

8.

Let *Bigots* preach up what imposture hath taught,
    And *Falshood* promulge her decrees ;
Be *mine* the Religion to act as I ought,
    Whilst *hypocrites* act as they please.

9.

In *Humility's* vale I will hide from the storm,
    From *Folly's* vile minions apart ;
What *Justice* requires I will strive to perform,
    And *Mercy* shall dwell in my heart.

10. The

10.

The pupil of *Innocence*, *Friendſhip*, and *Peace*,

  My ſoul with *Benevolence* fraught ;

This life I will ſpend, and in *Wiſdom* increaſe,

  And *Reaſon* ſhall govern my thought.

11.

The victims of *Sorrow* ſhall call me their friend,

  I feel, and partake, of their woe ;

To the whole human race my *good-will* ſhall extend,

  And I 'll wiſh I had *more* to beſtow.

12.

Though injur'd by villains, though *Fortune* may frown,

  I 'll patiently bear with my lot ;

Let *Gold* be the miſer's, *Content* is my own,

  And *Vanity* flies from my cot.

13.

Thus I 'll live and be good, and not envy the Great

  What pleaſures they borrow from art ;

They may think what they pleaſe, but *Ambition's* a cheat,

  That hardens and cankers the heart.

14. Harm-

14.

Harmlefs *Mirth*, now and then, fhall a moment em‑
    ploy

  With a friend o'er a temperate glafs ;

What 's *lawful* in pleafure I 'll fearlefs enjoy,

  As through this dark lab'rinth I pafs.

15.

The day will foon come to refign up my breath,

  And *Faith* now directs me the road

To pafs through the vale, the deep fhadows of *Death*,

  To *Virtue's* eternal abode.

————————

EPIGRAM.

E P I G R A M.

To-MORROW, fays Dick, I 'll caft follies away ;
  Forfake ev'ry vice ; my vile habits reprefs :
But make, my good friend, a beginning to-day ;
  If *living* to-morrow, thy work will be lefs.

DECEITFUL

DECEITFUL CELIA,

A PASTORAL BALLAD,

WRITTEN IN 1778.

1.

BEWARE of Love, ye gentle fwains,
That woful bane of reft ;
Its madden'd hope, its poignant pains,
Will forely grieve the breaft.

2.

With foul fincere I once ador'd
A felfifh, artful, maid ;
And, by blind Paffion overpow'r'd,
I thought my love re-paid.

3. Love's

3.

Love's tender look she well could feign,
  Affect its melting tone ;
And thus deceiv'd a simple swain
  Whose heart was all her own.

4.

This rural cot I strove to rear,
  My little flock improv'd ;
Fix'd ev'ry thought, with anxious care,
  On her I dearly lov'd.

5.

This orchard owns no rival nigh,
  'Twas planted for her sake ;
The wish to please my charmer's eye
  Kept all my soul awake.

6.

But Lubin came, and quaintly told
  His tale with studious art;
Then shew'd a purse well-cramm'd with gold,
  And won my Celia's heart.

7. Adore

7.

Adore that gold, ungrateful maid,
  Be rich, and hug thyself;
Thou soon wilt feel thy heart betray'd
  By that vile miser's pelf.

8.

My partial Muse, with effort warm,
  Made thee the darling theme;
I saw thee deck'd with ev'ry charm
  In Love's bewitching dream.

9.

How have I gaz'd on thy bright eyes!
  With transport felt thy kiss!
How did my soul in thee comprize
  The whole of earthly bliss!

10.

Chang'd in a moment, thou, by stealth,
  Art in old Lubin's arms;
Hast made, for pomp and sordid wealth,
  A sale of all thy charms.

11. Wrong'd

11.

Wrong'd haft thou thus an honeft heart,

 Where Love's warm ardour glow'd ;

Where, fprung from truth in ev'ry part,

 The ftream unfullied flow'd.

12.

Soon fhalt thou mourn thy joylefs fate,

 Thy worthlefs choice deplore,

Shalt weep forlorn, but weep too late ;

 Love's day returns no more.

13.

Lubin's cold heart yields no relief

 When cares thy bofom gall ;

But all true lovers mock thy grief,

 And triumph in thy fall.

14.

Whilft, cur'd of Love's fantaftic woes,

 Wife Colin lives at reft ;

In Reafon finds a foft repofe,

 And comfort fills his breaft.

15. And,

15.

And, free from wealth's attendant ſtrife,
    He lives a rural ſwain ;
Enjoys in peace the ſhepherd's life
    Inglorious on the plain.

EPITAPH ON A POET.

HERE let a *Bard* unenvied reſt,
Where no dull *Critick* dares moleſt;
Eſcap'd from the familiar curſe
Of *threadbare coat* and *empty purſe*,
From rough *Bumbailiffs*, threat'ning *Duns*,
From ſtupid *Pride's* deteſted ſons,
From all thoſe peſt'ring ills of life;
From worſe than all—*A ſcolding wife.*

A WELSH

A WELSH PROVERBIAL RHIME,

Common in Glamorgan.

PÀN glywer y Môr yn crochlefain yn fflin,

A'r cwmwl yn dew am bèn Caftell Penllin,

Os gwîr yr hên ddjareb, mae cawad o wlaw,

Yn magu'n yr wybren, a'i fyrthiad gerllaw.

T R A N S L A T I O N.

Which Mr. GROSE has thus introduced in his Account

of Penlline Caftle, in Glamorgan. Vol. VII. p. 90,

2d edit.

" Penlline, like diverfe other elevated fpots, affords

" a kind of prognoftic for the weather, fpecified in the

" following verfes."

W H E N

WHEN the hoarfe waves of *Severn* are fcreaming
   aloud,

And *Penlline's* lofty caftle 's involv'd in a cloud,

If true the old proverb, a fhower of rain

Is brooding above, and will foon drench the plain.

Penlline Caftle is the property of Mifs GWINNETTE,
*who has lately built an elegant new houfe, in the caftle
ftile, clofe to the ruin. She has fhewn her good tafte
in not demolifhing the old caftle, fome of the walls of
which are conftructed in the manner of the old Roman
walls of* SEGONTIUM, *by the Town of* CAERNARVON.

A PAS.

A PASTORAL SONG,

To the old Welſh Tune—" Break of Day."

1.

To where yon lofty mountain

   Afcends with eafy fwell,

Whence many a cryſtal fountain,

   Runs purling down the dell ;

Whilſt from yon Eaſt the morning

   Calls forth its purple charms,

From foreign ſhores returning,

   I fly to Sally's arms.

Through

Through midnight's gloomy shadows

   I forc'd my labour'd way,

      With eager hafte,

      O'er wild and wafte,

   A foe to long delay:

Now joyful in the meadows,

   Where fmiles the lovely May,

      With choral fong,

      The pinion'd throng,

   Proclaim the *break of day.*

2.

The blackbird's mellow chaunting

   Would fain detain my feet;

But, where my Sally 's wanting,

   No blifs can be complete.

Ye flow'rets of the valley,

   My fighs are not for you;

I 'm haftening to my Sally,

   And bid your fweets adieu.

No

No pleasures from my fairest
  Can lead my thoughts astray ;
    Th' enamel'd ground,
    The groves around,
  Enrob'd in Spring's array :
I soon shall meet my dearest,
  Then, Grief, thou must away,
    When Love supplies,
    From her sweet eyes,
  My brighter *break of day.*

WINTER

WINTER INCIDENTS.

WRITTEN IN 1777.

BLEAK Winter comes with wrathful roar.
Exclude the tyrant! fhut the door,
And let us blunt his nipping gale
With blazing hearths, with fparkling ale,
And lead the fullen hours along
With tale of old and mirthful fong.

No feather'd fongfter tunes a lay,
To cheer the fhort, the joylefs, day;
Yon mournful blackbird mopes alone,
Has quite forgot his mellow tone;
How mute yon linnet on the thorn!
No joyous lark falutes the morn;

VOL. I.   G   The

The fcreech-owl tells her doleful tale

Where warbled once the nightingale;

Wild geefe with clamours fill the fky,

Their clank proclaims the tempeft nigh;

Swans, fearful of the polar gales,

Seek fhelter in *Silurian* vales * ;

The fea-gull in the meadow fcreams,

And wood-cocks haunt lone thicket-ftreams;

Rude winds from hills *Brigantian* † blow,

And from their pinions fhake the fnow;

Whilft trembling ftars, intenfely bright,

Pour all their fulgence on the night;

The breeze with gellid rigour teems,

And túrns to rock the languid ftreams,

---

* *Seek fhelter in* Silurian *vales.*] In hard Winters the Vale of *Glamorgan* (part of the ancient *Siluria)* is frequented by many fwans, from whence, I believe, is unknown. They always depart when the frofts are over.

† *Hills* Brigantian.] *Brigantium* was the ancient name of the Northern parts of England.

Whilft,

Whilst, from its fount on yonder hill,

Unfetter'd runs the rapid rill.

The village boys with morn awake

To trace the furface of the lake,

And, thoughtlefs, run at paffion's call,

In flipp'ry paths, where many fall :

The juft refemblance let me fcan ;

'Tis *rafh defire*, unthinking man ;

Though feeming joy thy wifh attends,

The fell deceit in ruin ends.

Obferve yon prattling lifper ftrain,

To roll the fnow-ball o'er the plain ;

So mifers heap, with fore turmoil,

What never can re-pay their toil.

As trudging home befide the brook,

With health redundant in his look,

Yon fturdy farmer blows his nails,

And his unluckly lot bewails,

Not deftin'd, like the drunken 'fquire,

To lounge before the parlour fire ;

Man,

Man, difcontented with his fate,
Ne'er fees the folly till too late.

Now village curs, with echo'd howl,
Scare from her haunt the plaintive owl.
Foreboding billows loudly roar,
And cloath in foam the rocky fhore ;
We guard againft the pelting rain,
'Twill foon with fury fweep the plain.

Wife Induftry, thou canft defy
The terrors of a wintry fky ;
When ftorms are fierce, and billows rude,
Thou canft with eafe their force elude ;
With fmiling plenty ftore thy fhed ;
In warmth repofe thy pillow'd head ;
Pile high thy crackling hearth, and tune
A cheerful fong to *rofy June*.

Important in his elbow chair,
The village fage, in filver'd hair,
With felf-applauding glee, repeats
His well-known tale of youthful feats :

He was a very *blade*, he fays,

Not like your *louts* of modern days ;

He won at wreftling many a prize ;

Could nicely box a neighbour's eyes ;

And, 'twas allow'd by all the town,

Could fairly drink a *Parfon* down.

Thus, oddly thus, we grafp at fame,

Puff to the world an odious name.

How little is it underftood,

That, to be *great*, we muft be *good*.

  Hark ! from yon dell what frightful found

Spreads thund'ring horror all around !

Sweet thrufh ! firft herald of the Spring,

Joy warm'd my foul to hear thee fing ;

What time appear'd the primrofe pale,

Near my lone arbour in the dale ;

Where warbled wild thy carols gay,

Prophetic of the lovely May ;

Now, bleeding from thy mortal wound,

I view thee, flutt'ring, on the ground ;

' But

But cruelty could ne'er appall
The ruthlefs heart that doom'd thy fall.

Thou, that in blood canft thus delight,
Steel well thy foul, court fame, and fight,
With well-directed cannon balls
Knock down ten thoufand harmlefs Gauls,
Drink human gore, and laugh thy fill
At Him who faid, " *Thou fhalt not kill.*"
I, who for *Britain*, *Franee*, and *Spain*,
Crave peace from Heav'n, and crave again,
Unmindful of the puffs of Fame,
Weep, and deteft the warrior's- name.
If, in life's road, it be my chance
To meet a *brother* born in *France*,
A ftranger in the fangs of grief,
Where no kind hand affords relief;
He, though *contending cannons* roar,
Shall open find my friendly door;
And, fpite of all that *Kings* command,
Find in my cot his *native land*,

My

My peaceful cot, fecluded far

From Hell-born rage of ruthlefs war.

   Nature each cruel thought repels,

Rare is that heart where nature dwells;

Where foft compaffion is combin'd

With ev'ry motion of the mind;

Where genial feelings form the man

On fearlefs *Love's* eternal plan.

   What midnight horrors, raging high,

Affemble in the ftormy fky !

The forky lightnings now defcend;

But reft in peace, my foreign friend;

They thunder harmlefs o'er thy head,

Not level'd at this humble fhed :

No dread we feel, an anger'd GOD

Finds here no vile *Oppreffor's* rod :

Though 'tis thy lot awhile to part

From each dear object of thy heart,

All Nature, at *one* GREAT Command,

Shall guard them with parental hand;

Thou

Thou ſhalt behold again with joy,

Thy prattling girl, thy liſping boy;

And, doom'd in grief no more to roam,

Enjoy through life thy native home.

D A-

D A M O N'S   F A R E W E L.

A   S O N G.

1.

Am I doom'd, O! my Phillis, no more to purſue

My claim, once allow'd, in thy heart ?

Muſt I bid thee, my charmer, for ever adieu ?

With my life's only happineſs part ?

No tongue can, alas ! the wild agonies tell

That rend my ſad ſoul thus to bid thee *farewel.*

2.

How ſad to recall the paſt moments of bliſs,

When thy look ſpoke thee conſtant and kind !

When I hung on thy lips in a rapturous kiſs ;

A monarch, and more, in my mind !

G 5   But

.But no more muſt this heart with love's ecſtacy.
    ſwell ;

My Phillis, how cruel! now bids me *farewel*.

3.

What viſions of happineſs blaz'd on my view,
    When I, thoughtleſs, gave way to my love!
But Phillis conſented, and ſwore to be true;
    'Twas an oath by the Powers above.
Now ſable deſpair muſt all comfort expel;
She gives the command, I muſt bid her *farewel*.

4.

To wander, to weep, through life's deſart alone,
    Muſt hence be my comfortleſs fate ;
My ſorrows unpity'd, unheeded my moan, .
    Like the turtle, depriv'd of his mate.
O ! Death ! when wilt thou my deep anguiſh
    diſpel ?
'Tis death, worſe than death, to bid Phillis *farewel*.

5. FARE-

5.

Farewel, my dear Phillis ; may Fortune befriend

   Thy wiſhes, and wait on thee ſtill !

May the joys of all Nature thy moments attend,

   Like ſlaves that ſubmit to thy will !

On thy name haplefs Damon will dolefully dwell,

Whilſt, whelm'd in diſtraction, he bids thee—*farewel.*

L I B E R T Y,

A   S O N G.

1.

WHILST the whining Lover flies

To some far-sequester'd cave,

Bootless there to vent his sighs

To the storms that loudly rave;

Liberty, thy charms I sing;

Let the rounds with echo ring.

2.

Subject to no tyrant sway,

Saucy love, or despot king,

Free as air I pass the day,

And give sneaking Care the fling:

Free-born Britons, join with me;

'Tis the song of *Liberty*,

3. Love,

3.

Love, 'tis true, defpotic rules

 On Britannia's verdant plains ;

Turns Philofophers to fools;

 How they hug their galling chains !

Slaves that, fcorning to be free,

Boaft their lofs of *Liberty.*

4.

Long I bore Belinda's yoke,

 Long I ftruggled in her toils ;

From her gaol at laft I broke ;

 Freed my heart from fore turmoils.

Now, poor Love, I laugh at thee ;

And am blefs'd with *Liberty.*

5.

Soul-exalting *Liberty,*

 Source of peace and fweet content,

Nature, ever fond of thee,

 Rambles o'er thy wide extent:

And

And the Muſe exerts her glee,

When ſhe ſings of *Liberty*.

6.

Fill the glaſs—another ſong—

⸱ How yon Lover ſlinks away !

Bear the chorus briſk along ;

Mirth demands the ſportive lay :⸱

Toaſt around the bliſsful trine,

Friendſhip, Liberty, and Wine.⸱

O N

ON LOVE.

WRITTEN IN 1777.

I.

I HOP'D, within this lonely bow'r,

   In penfive eafe reclin'd,

To fteal from care one peaceful hour,

   With fóng to foothe my mind;

An old, but yet unconquer'd, thrill

   Deprives my thought of reft;

I feel the flame of paffion ftill

   Unfmother'd in my breaft.

2. Love,

2.

Love, bold intruder, fince my lay
   Derives a theme from thee,
My bow'r approach; but drive away
   That fiend Hypocrify:
Come fimple, as in days of yore,
   Untried in feats of art:
Attend me thus, I 'll own thy pow'r;
   Admit thee to my heart.

3.

Yet there Sufpicion's careful eye
   Shall watch thy varied wiles;
Nor dare, in wild'ring hope, rely
   On bright bewitching fmiles:
I know thy wifh, 'twas once betray'd;
   In Falfhood's fetters caught;
Though living ftill, it feels afraid,
   And wears the fhield of thought.

4. Art

4.

Art thou that foft unchanging love,
   Affliction's beſt relief?
That ſmiling cherub, from above,
   That cheers defponding grief?
That ſweetly deals the fov'reign balm
   When Anguiſh tears the breaſt?
That can the rankled feelings calm,
   And charm the foul to reſt?

5.

Or art thou not, in borrow'd form,
   The pamper'd imp of Luſt,
Or ſpawn of Av'rice, that vile worm,
   That feeds on filthy duſt?
Be gone! the deep deceit I fear,
   Hence wing thy ſpeedy flight!
I ſee thy cloven foot appear,
   Though clad in robes of light.

6. I faw

6.

I saw the vi'let of the vale

   Expand in early bloom ;

Morn sent abroad the fanning gale,

   Fraught with its rich perfume ;

But, courting Noon's refulgent hour,

   How vapid falls thy head !

Thy transient sweets, neglected flow'r,

   Are gone—for ever fled.

7.

Just emblem of my Celia's love !

   Bright was its morning ray ;

'Twas fancy'd once the Turtle Dove,

   But vanish'd soon away :

Her eyes were drawn by golden views,

   For wealth she sorely pin'd ;

And I had nothing, but the Muse,

   To please her selfish mind.

8. Say,

8.

Say, Celia, whence th' unusual gloom
    That hangs upon thy brows?
I saw thy cheek with beauty bloom,
    With Health's delicious rose:
He, that thy faithless hand obtain'd,
    A Miser sorely crofs'd,
Slights all thy charms, no pelf he gain'd,
    And all his joys are lost.

9.

Mad passions, that I felt with pain,
    My thoughts no longer vex;
Nor shall this bosom bleed again
    For thy deceitful sex:
Yet, to sublimer love awake,
    My soul, with warm embrace,
Can, in its wide expansion, take
    The whole of human race.

10. In-

10.

Infpirer of th' angelic lay,

 Dove-ey'd Benevolence;

I join the few that feek thy way,

 Warm'd by thy nobler fenfe:

Plant all thy feelings in my breaft;

 Thy fervent wifh impart:

Of all its hidden fprings poffefs'd,

 Reign Monarch of my heart.

———————

T H E

THE POWER OF INNOCENCE.

From the Welsh.

I HAVE felt the rough North, and fierce fangs of
　　the froſt,

On the bed of diſeaſe by ſharp anguiſh been toſt;

Theſe agoniz'd nerves were once horribly pain'd,

When long on my fleſh the live embers remain'd;

A torture ſtill keener corroded my heart,

From my love's darling objeĉts doom'd ſadly to part;

All theſe have I felt, all with patience I bore,

And, if *Duty* commands, I can ſtruggle with more;

There 's a pain ſtill feverer, and bear it who can?

The ſtinging reproach of a ſenſible man;

'Tis *Innocence* can, without ſhedding one tear;

She can ſing in the flames, and triumphantly bear.

S O L I T U D E.

From the Welsh *.

WRITTEN IN 1789.

SAY, why, my friend, would'ſt thou perſuade
Thy Bard to quit his tranquil ſhade ?
He dwells contented with his lot,
Hid from the world in humble cot ;
And, heedleſs of the glare of wealth,
. Finds all he wants in peace and health ;
With hopes, when well-matur'd by age,
To find himſelf a rural Sage.

---

* From the Author's own Welſh ; and it is always ſo where
no other name is given.

Sweet

Sweet Solitude has peerlefs charms,

Where Virtue's glow the bofom warms;

Where waken'd Confcience feels no pain,

And Reafon breaks dull Folly's chain;

Where Tafte informs th' obfervant eye,

That can bright Nature's charms defcry;

And where the ftrong, enlighten'd mind

Can in itfelf fweet converfe find;

Can talk with Truth, too little known,

That in the Confcience rears her throne.

He, that avoids the jar of ftrife,

Spends here unknown his quiet life;

The *Mufe*, with *Fancy's* plaftic pow'r,

Will vifit oft his lonely bow'r;

Inftruct him in the tuneful art,

Illume his mind, refine his heart;

And *Wifdom* fhall his thought expand,

His foul is all at her Command:

His breaft, where once wild Paffion ftorm'd,

Is by Adverfity reform'd;

Blefs'd

Blefs'd in th' event, his grateful mind

Adores the rod, and ftands refign'd,

Submits, with reverential awe,

To gracious Heav'n's unerring law.

Reftor'd by this to mental eafe,

He feels the lore of Nature pleafe;

And lays his head in downy reft,

Meek Innocence, upon thy breaft;

Yet hears, with forrow, from afar,

The madden'd world's eternal war;

Sees where the blamelefs heart is broke

By dire Oppreffion's galling yoke;

Where *Kings*, that *fiends incarnate* reign,

With human carnage load the plain;

For this his bofom heaves the figh;

For this the tear ftreams from his eye.

O! when fhall man from difcord ceafe?

Rul'd by thy laws, thou *Prince of Peace*,

Obey thy mandates from above,

And own thy reign of endlefs *Love*.

Behold,

Behold, on *Afric's* beach, alone,

Yon fire that weeps with bitter moan ;

She, that his life once truly blefs'd,

Is torn for ever from his breaft,

And, *fcourged*, where *Britifh Monarchs* reign,

Calls for his aid, but calls in vain ;

His fons, on *Slav'ry's* fhamelefs land,

Now bleed beneath a *Villain's* hand ;

Their writhing frames how forely gall'd !

Still *Britons* muft be *Chriftians* call'd—

Their groans the wide horizon fill !

Vile *Britons !* 'tis your *Senate's* will—

I ceafe.—thofe cruelties affright

A Mufe that fhudders at the fight.

F R A G M E N T.

From the Welſh.

LET wealth, let fame, thoſe dazzling gifts of
    Fate,
Bleſs all the wayward ſons of pomp and ſtate ;
Be mine the riches of a ſoul refin'd,
The heart benevolent, the ſpotleſs mind,
To Heav'n's unerring will, in humble hope, re-
    ſign'd.

T H E

T H E   D R E A M,

A   P A S T O R A L.

From the Welſh.

I.

A H ! where art thou flown, lovely dream of de-
    light?
Thy moments of blifs are all vaniſh'd away;
All blended, alas ! with the deep ſhades of night;
    Why wak'd my fond thought to thy treacherous
    day ?
How fulgent the morn ! how refreſhing the gale !
    May's melody warbled around in the grove;
With Phillis I walk'd, arm in arm, o'er the vale,
    Her ſmile, her ſoft look, ſpoke the language of
    love.

H 2   The

The loud roar of thunder, the lightning's fierce
    gleam,
Awake me to grief, all my blifs was a *Dream*.

2.

In the bloom-fpangled mantle of Beauty confefs'd,
    May charms the rapt eyes o'er the landfcape
      around ;
In delicate verdure the thickets are drefs'd ;
    Hills, woodlands, and vales, with fweet mufic
      refound ;
I fit with my charmer beneath the green thorn,
    Where fweet rural fcenes open full to the view ;
Or walk with our flocks through the dews of the
    morn ;
    Cares quit my glad foul, I now bid them adieu.
The Mufe quickly grafp'd at the rapturous theme,
Of happinefs fung—but her fong was a *Dream*.

3. How

3.

How charming the fcene! 'tis my favourite vale,

 Where I firſt found the Mufe in gay fancies of

  youth;

Where firſt to my Phillis I utter'd my tale

 Of paſſion, of love, in the language of truth;

Here firſt with rapt foul of her beauties I fung;

 Here firſt for my charmer in folitude mourn'd;

I now hear, with tranſport, her faultering tongue

 Confeſs the warm wiſh, and my love is return'd.

Ah! joy from my foul has withdrawn its bright

  beam,

The phantom is flown with the treacherous *Dream.*

4.

How lovely my Fair! how enchanting her mien!

 How throbs my fond heart whilſt I gaze on her

  charms!

In her all the graces of nature are feen;

 And all that the foul of a lover alarms:

         Her

Her fweet rofy lips with warm rapture I kifs;

   I feel the ftrong flame in my bofom arife ;

My thoughts are all whelm'd in a torrent of blifs,

   My fenfes involv'd in a tender furprize.

Love's joys I poffefs in a blifsful extreme—

'Twas a fhade that all vanifh'd, poffefs'd in a

   Dream.

5.

. How oft have I languifh'd alone in this bow'r,

   Attempting to fly from the fting of Defpair !

Sore bled my poor heart when Defpondency's hour

   Led on the fharp ranklings of Anguifh and Care :

My love I declar'd whilft the witneffing tear

   Was treated with fcorn by the pitilefs maid :

But now fhe relents, and my amiable Fair

   Has all my paft grief in one moment repaid.

No longer I ftrive againft Love's mighty ftream ;

How glad ! how rejoic'd !—how deceiv'd ! in a

   Dream.

6. I once,

6.

I once, with my flocks, unincumber'd with cares,
   Could whistle and sing through the Summer's long
     day;
My roses I cultur'd, or grafted my pears;
   How pass'd with delight my sweet moments
     away!
But pleasure no longer inhabits my breast;
   My lambs, my sweet garden, afford me no joy;
I ramble the wilds, vainly searching for rest,
   And ev'ry warm thought on my Phillis employ.
Last night, with the smile of Love's tender esteem,
My charmer complied—but complied in a *Dream.*

7.

My joys are all dead, and, enchanted, no more
   I gaze on my Phillis, and dwell on her charms;
Return, lovely dream, and, in pity, restore
   My Fair-one again to my wide-op'ning arms;

O! bring

O! bring her again to this nook of the vale,

  On Love's tender errands delightfully bent ;

And, whilſt I repeat my ſoft amorous tale,

  Illumine her looks with the ſmile of conſent ;

And let me, whilſt buſied on this happy ſcheme,

Eternally ſleep, and eternally *dream*.

SONNET.

S O N N E T.

From the Welſh.

LOVE is a wild confuſion of the ſoul,
To brave its pow'r enfeebled Reaſon fails ;
The deſpot reigns with abſolute controul,
With ſtrong enchantment ev'ry thought aſſails :
Where genial ſenſibility prevails,
Unguarded paſſions catch its ardent fire,
And, fewel'd high by Hope's alluring tales,
Inflame the wilder'd mind with ſtrange deſire ;
It leaves in joyleſs calms th' unfavour'd breaſt,
Where ſordid ſelf locks up the callous heart,
But in the tender feeling lives confeſs'd
In viſions bright that thrilling joys impart ;
Song ſtrives to paint it, efforts vainly ſhewn,
The wordleſs heart muſt feel, or Love can ne'er be
known.

H 5   IDEAL

I D E A L - G R I E F.

'Rwyf ôcunydd yn rhoi ièn i'r Byd,
A gado i 'mryd ynfydu,
A'r pxen, a'i aebos, fal y faeth,
O 'r bunan ca:th yn tyfu.

This world I flander, to my fhame,
Nor ftrive my paffions once to tame :
Sharp ills I feel, but all, I find,
Spring from my own unmanly mind.

I.

NOW darknefs envelopes the grove,
And dies the laft gleam of the Weft,
Whilft o'er the rough defart I rove,
Indulging fad thoughts in my breaft ;
Nor whirlwinds that fternly refound,
Nor billows that irefully roll,
All Winter's grim horrors around,
Can equal the ftorm in my foul.

5   2. I

2.

I climb the rude rocks in the dark,
  Till, wearied, I fall on the ground;
On days that are flown I remark,
  Whilſt galling reflections abound;
I dwell on the falſhoods of Art;
  Remember the tales I believ'd;
And, weeping, deplore my fond heart,
  In Love and in Friendſhip deceiv'd.

3.

All comfort is flown from my ſight,
  But Solitude's gloomy relief,
I ramble forlorn in the night,
  To ruminate wild on my grief:
With Memory prompting the ſigh,
  With feelings that Villainy ſmote,
Vile *man*, from thy dwellings I fly
  To the caves of the mountain remote.

4. My

4.

My foul with defpondency fraught

   Gave way to thofe phantoms of care,

When the *Angel* of *Reafon*, I thought,

   Thus utter'd a voice in my ear :

" Blind mortal, what makes thee complain,

   " To Frailty thus yielding thy mind ;

" Mad Fancy creates all thy pain,

   " Or Pride with wild Paffion combin'd."

THE

THE LINE OF BEAUTY.

The Author was, one evening, invited to be of a party to see the new-laid-out pleasure-grounds of a Gentleman. —The walks waved regularly along the rectilinear fences with very minute spirality, and crossed the ground at right angles, dividing the laboriously-levelled lawn into parts exactly square and equal. Clumps of pine and flowering shrubs, of studied rotundity, bestudded the smooth-shaven green at regular distances; and the stiffest formalities prevailed every where. The Gardener who attended talked much of the LINE OF BEAUTY. " Curse " your Line of Beauty," exclaimed the Bard. —" You must " write a song on the subject," said one of the Ladies. " By G— you must," cried a young Clergyman, " and " the LINE OF BEAUTY must conclude every stanza : " find rhymes if you can."—" I insist upon it," said another Lady, " that the Reverend SWEARER should have

" a con-

" *a conspicuous place in the song.*"—*After an hour's re-tirement, the Author joined his good-humoured company with the following verses* :

1.

To view dull Fashion's boasted feats,
  Her formal clumps of pine, fir,
Her frizzled walks, her painted seats,
  And all things vastly fine, fir.
One ev'ning on her lawn we met;
  I tell the story true t' ye ;
Our Bard look'd round, and, in a pet,
  He curs'd the *Line of Beauty.*

2.

This Bard was sure an oddity,
  Or something quite as bad, fir ;
At crambo rhyming who, but he !
  We thought the fellow mad, fir.

Here !

Here I take the fong—I think 'twill give.

His mind's uncommon hue t' ye— '

He Fafhion hates—and, as I live,

Lampoons *her line of beauty.*

3.

" From empyrëan realms of light,

" Where Vice affrighted views thee;

" Look down, HOGARTH, from envy'd height,

" And fee where fools abufe thee—

" Ye, led by *Tafte,* obferve this walk;

" 'Tis dullnefs full in view t' ye;

" Yon blockhead's boaft, whofe idle talk

" Defames the *line of beauty.*

4.

" Ye, taught in Art's pedantic fchools,

" Ye flaves of ftupid Fafhion,

" Hafte! banifh hence your lifelefs rules;

" They put us in a paffion.

" Ye break through Taſte, through Nature's laws,

   " They bid a long adieu t' ye ;

" And leave the Bard an urgent cauſe

   " To curſe your *line of beauty*.

5.

" But would ye ſtudy Nature's charms,

   " On plains *Silurian* greet her ;

" She flies at PIERCEFIELD * to your arms,

   " On ITTON's † lawns you 'll meet her ;

" There, haunting woods and vallies green,

   " She 'll with a ſmile ſalute ye ;

" Her fingers mark each lovely ſcene

   " With perfeＣt *lines of beauty*.

---

  * PIERCEFIELD.] The celebrated ſeat of GEORGE SMITH, Eſq.

  † ITTON COURT.] The ſeat of JOHN CURRY, Eſq. The furrounding landſcapes, though of a different charaＣter from thoſe at PIERCEFIELD, are extremely beautiful.

6. " Be-

6.

" Behold yon mountain's airy flope,

   " Yon winding vale romantic,

" Where Fancy takes unbounded fcope ;

   " Dull *Critics* think her frantic ;

" Unfetter'd there fhe dwells with Tafte,

   " And lends her friendly clue t' ye ;

" See, pencil'd o'er the flow'ry wafte,

   " Her fportive *lines of beauty.*

7.

" In vain ye ply this *naked* ART,

   " Your *ftudied forms* are teazing ;

" 'Tis NATURE only wins the heart ;

   " Her looks are ever pleafing ;

" *Simplicity's* unrivall'd grace

   " Has charms for ever new t' ye ;

" Then view fweet ANNA's lovely face,

   " And blefs the *line of beauty.*

8. " I

8.

" I heard the naughty Parſon ſwear,

" The Ladies made wry faces ;

" He from that practice muſt forbear,

" An oath his cloth diſgraces ;

" Avoid th' infectious touch of *Sin*,

" Its venom will pollute ye ;

" Sweet Happineſs is found within.

" The CHRISTIAN *line of beauty*.

9.

" To talk of *Sin*, you think me now

" Some cloud-exploring *Myſtic* ;

" Some *Quaker*, fond of *thee* and *thou*,

" Some preacher *Methodiſtic* :

" However you nick-name the Bard,

" He ſeeks the paths of Duty ;

" And thinks it wiſdom to regard

" RELIGION's *line of beauty!*"—

T O

TO THE NIGHTINGALE,

A PASTORAL.

From the Welsh.

1.

PEACEFUL Night now reigns around,
   Gives to solemn silence all,
Save yon warbler's tuneful found,
   And the distant water-fall.

2.

Fond of Quiet's milder scene,
   Let me walk this lonely vale ;
Whilst amid her thicket green,
   Sings the mournful Nightingale.

3. Musing.

3.

Muſing here I walk alone,

　Fancy points my devious way ;

Liſt'ning to thy melting tone,

　Songſter of departing day.

4.

Here the brooklet purls along,

　Here I feel a warm delight ;

Where thy ſweet unrivall'd ſong

　Charms the ſtillneſs of the night.

5.

Now, depriv'd of balmy ſleep,

　By the tender cares of Love ;

I with thee my vigils keep,

　Midnight warbler of the grove.

6.

Oft I walk the dewy lawn,

　When, unſeen in matted thorn,

Trills thy muſic to the dawn,

　Early minſtrel of the morn.

7. Pleas'd

7.

Pleas'd I liſten on the plain,

Where my ſportive lambkins play ;

Whilſt thy voice, with varied ſtrain,

Fills the chorus of the day *.

8.

Oft I leave the world behind,

Often bend my pathleſs way

Through this dale, with penſive mind,

And attend thy ſoothing lay.

9.

Often, hid within the grove,

Let me try thy tuneful art ;

Whilſt the ſweet concerns of Love,

Revel in my thrilling heart.

---

* The Nightingale ſings by DAY as well as by NIGHT. It is
rather ſtrange that this faƈt has not been obſerved by any of
our Engliſh Poets.

EPITAPH

E P I T A P H

ON AN OLD-FASHIONED FELLOW.

H E R E lies, beneath this verdant fod,

One that believ'd there was a *God* :

He ev'ry day the *Bible* read,

What fancies fill'd the fellow's head!

He *Pomp* detefted, pity'd *Kings*,

And thought *high Titles* worthlefs things ;

Thought *Beaus* and *Wits*, with huge pretence,

Had not one grain of common fenfe ;

To grafp at *wealth* was not his rule,

He, furely, was an arrant fool ;

And to the *Poor*, imprudent, gave

What wifer heads would ftrive to fave ;

He

He always gave uncommon fcope

To thofe old whimfies *Faith* and *Hope* ;

So much our lov'd purfuits would blame,

We almoft felt a little fhame ;

Now, dead and gone, we blefs the day,

He ftands no longer in the way.

———————————

S E L F I S H N E S S.

SOME boaſt themſelves immenſely good,

They never drench their hands in blood;

Are loath to ſteal their daily bread;

Nor once invade a neighbour's bed.

We muſt applaud their blameleſs courſe;

But ſay, from what unfailing ſource

Thoſe brilliant virtues ever flow ?—

The *Gallows* here, and *Hell* below.

'Tis not the ſoul on virtue bent,

But ſelfiſh fear of puniſhment:

Give Heav'n to theſe, and all is well;

The *friendleſs* GOD may go to Hell;

May burn, where fiends inſult his name,

Unpity'd in th' eternal flame.

THE

THE HAPPY FARMER.

A PASTORAL.

Inscribed to the GLAMORGAN *Agricultural Society.*

I.

I LIVE on my farm in a beautiful vale,
Ye lovers of Nature attend to my tale ;
No pride or ambition find room in my breast,
Those venomous foes of contentment and rest ;
From sound, healthy sleep I rise up ev'ry morn,
To toil in my fields with my cattle and corn,
And prefer, whilst of rural employments I sing,
The life of a *Farmer* to that of a *King*.

2.

On the fruits of my labour I look with delight,

My meadows are weedlefs, and gladden the fight;

The flocks in my paflures are fair to behold,

Fine cows with large udders replenifh my fold;

My fields yield abundance, in tillage complete,

Good barley, rich clover, and excellent wheat;

I the feafons attend, through their changeable round,

In toils that with Plenty's rich bleffings are crown'd.

3.

My houfe is convenient, and whiten'd all o'er,

An arbour of jeffamine fronting the door;

My flourifhing orchard abundantly bears

Fine plumbs, golden-pippins, and bergamot pears;

The rofe, the fweet pink, in my garden are found,

Where dainties of health for my table abound;

My mind, when fatigu'd, here I often unbend,

Perufe a good book, or converfe with a friend.

4. With

4.

With rural amufements, in fober delight,

I brighten my thoughts, their long labours requite;

And over my ftubbles, when harveft is done,

I range in the morn with my dog and my gun;

Now courfe the fleet hare on the fern-cover'd hill,

Or angle for trout in a neighbouring rill;

And fometimes at eve, to enliven my foul,

I fing with my friend o'er a temperate bowl.

5.

Where flocks and large herds in my paftures are feen,

The cowflips, or daify, befpangle the green;

I view my gay lambs nimbly frolic and play,

Whilft under their feet fpring the beauties of May;

Whilft, joyful, obferving my flourifhing corn,

The blackbird and linnet fing loud on the thorn:

Nor would I my peaceful employments lay down,

Or quit my green fields, for the pomp of a crown.

I 2   6. To

6.

To Providence grateful, I pity the poor,

Nor drive them in fadnefs away from my door ;

Befriending my neighbours, I do all I can

To act the good part of a fenfible man :

But fhould my griev'd confcience withhold its applaufe,

And blame me for trampling on Charity's laws ;

Then I mourn, and am penfive, upbraiding myfelf,

But not like the Mifer that whines for his pelf.

7.

Let lords of their high-founding titles be vain,

Let flaves of mean av'rice in cities remain,

Let thofe that court fame ramble wantonly far,

And feek it in fields of deteftable war ;

Let others go combat the rage of the feas,

And barter for lucre contentment and eafe ;

Whilft I live in innocence, fhelter'd from harm,

With Plenty and Peace on my flourifhing farm.

The

The Author thinks Paftoral a fpecies of Poetry that admits of as great a variety of fubjects as any other whatever; and that it is not neceffary, in the manner of modern Poets, to confine it folely to Love, and make his *whining fwains* ring perpetual changes on the names of

Hard-hearted Phillis,

And cold Amarillis, &c. &c.

A Poet in the character of a Shepherd, an occupation the moft proper of all others to reprefent primeval fimplicity and virtue, defcribes objects as they naturally prefent themfelves to the fenfes, and affect the mind; or utters fentiments that fpring from the fimple notions and inborn feelings of thofe that are unacquainted with the abftractions of philofophy, and the complex ideas derived from art. The fhepherd, who is the reprefentative and pupil of Nature, has, for his rural fong, at leaft as great a diverfity of themes as the more philofophic rhimer can boaft of; who, if he pleafes, may take to

I 3

him-

himſelf all the fine things of art, provided he leave the ſylvan Bard in full poſſeſſion of Nature.

There are ſome Critics " *who* (as Dr. Johnſon " obſerves, and the cap often fits his own head) *love* " *to talk of what they do not know*," that affect to ridicule Paſtoral Poetry: their miſconceptions of its nature are, moſt probably, occaſioned by the abſurd and unnatural rhapſodies that many have given us under the name of Paſtoral; the ſentiments highly fantaſtical, with deſcriptions of what no climate of this globe affords but that of *Grub-ſtreet*; where, among many rare things, are to be ſeen, the violet of March and the roſe of June blowing at the ſame time, as we are told by Mr. POPE, in his firſt Paſtoral:

Here, on green banks, the *bluſhing* vi'lets glow,
Here Weſtern winds on breathing roſes blow.
And, in the ſecond, he ſays,

The *Naiads* wept in ev'ry *wat'ry* bow'r,
And *Jove* conſented in a ſilent ſhow'r.

In

In the fourth we have the following lines :

Here fhall I try the fweet *Alexis'* ftrain,

That call'd the lift'ning *Dryads* to the plain ;

Thames heard the numbers as he flow'd along,

And bade his willows learn the moving fong.

What wonder is it that fuch *fweet* ALEXIS' *ftrains* as thefe, with the *curious* RULES given us by *Poet-makers*, who talk of their *Golden Age*, and we know not what, fhould induce many to think meanly of Paftoral Poetry.

It would, perhaps, not be amifs if our modern *Critics* and *Poets* would take into confideration the following maxim of the *Welfh Bards*, from their *Poetic Triades*.

Tri phrif anhepcor awen,

   Llygad yn gweled Anian,

   Calon yn teimlo Anian,

   A glewder a faidd gydfyned ag Anian.

The

The three primary and indifpenfable requifites of poetic genius are,

An eye that can fee Nature;

A heart that can feel Nature;

And a refolution that dares follow Nature.

Quære? Have any of the great *Manufacturers* of Poets, from the days of *Ariftotle* to the prefent time, ever faid any thing more to the purpofe? But the *Poetic Triades* will never emerge from their deep ob-fcurity in the *Welfh Language*: they contain fome of the moft juft, becaufe the moft natural, rules of Criticifm that are to be met with in any language.

————————

TRUE

TRUE HAPPINESS.

From the Welsh.

1.

THE wrinkled Miser loves to dwell
With Av'rice in her murky cell,
   To Care consigns his narrow soul ;
Light-hearted youths, in merry vein,
Assemble sportive on the plain,
   Whilst others quaff the mantling bowl ;
We mortals all in varied schemes employ
The visionary thought in blind pursuits of Joy.

2. I

2.

I feek nor wealth, nor youthful play,

Nor fottifh Mirth's unmeaning lay,

But, on my native plains alone,

I walk along the filent mead,

And tune in peace my rural reed,

To all the bufy world unknown;

I quit the crowd, fly far from hateful noife,

And feel my thoughful Mufe the fource of endlefs joys.

3.

Secluded thus in calm content,

On clofe purfuits of Nature bent,

I tuneful numbers lead along;

Whilft warm enamour'd thoughts arife,

Come, Virtue, from thy native fkies,

Be thou my theme of raptur'd fong.

We feel no joy from fordid Earth refin'd,

But where thy laws illume, and rule the willing mind.

THE

THE THRUSH.

1.

HOW void of care yon merry Thrush,

That tunes melodious on the bush,

That has no stores of wealth to keep,

No lands to plough, no corn to reap.

2.

His days, employ'd in lays of love,

Are spent within his native grove;

He never tempts the stormy main,

Nor deals in *blood* for filthy gain.

3.

He never frets for worthless things,

But lives in peace, and sweetly sings;

Enjoys the present with his mate,

Unmindful of to-morrow's fate.

4. Of

4.

Of true felicity poffefs'd,

He glides through life fupremely blefs'd;

And, for his daily meal, relies

On him whofe love the world fupplies.

5.

Rejoic'd he finds his morning fare,

His dinner lies—he knows not where—

Still, to th' unfailing hand, he chaunts,

His grateful fong, and never wants.

6.

He fits upon the bloomy fpray,

Joins harmlefs in the mirth of May;

Whilft *Man*, of Reafon's pow'r poffefs'd,

Feels afpic paffions rend his breaft.

7.

Sweet bird! from vain Ambition free,

Nor Pride, nor Envy dwell in thee;

And arts that innocence trepan

Are only known to *Hell* and *Man*.

5   8. What

8.

What art thou, *Man?*—a worthlefs elf;

A mafs of black infernal felf;

How joys thy foul to fling the dart,

Relentlefs, through thy *brother's* heart.

9.

Thy *fon's* poor orphan craves in vain,

His father fwallow'd by the main;

And, whilft of *want* thy *mother* dies,

Thy wealthy domes *infult* the fkies.

10.

Oh! change me, Nature!—let me be

The roughest *Bear* the world can fee;

The vileft of the *reptile* clan;

Be any thing but *cruel* Man.

C O N.

C O N T E N T,

A LYRIC PASTORAL.

I.

NOW morning meets my gladden'd eyes,

From healthful fleep I jocund rife,

With ftrength renew'd, and placid mind,

To relifh Nature's joys inclin'd,

I fpeed to meet the fragrant gale

That wantons in the dewy dale ;

And, as I pace the flow'ry way,

To fweet *Content* attune my lay.

2. How

2.

How clad with fmiles the vernal morn!

How gay the bloom-befpangled thorn!

The lark is up, the welkin rings,

And with his flock the fhepherd fings;

His notes a pleafing thrill impart;

They cheer my foul, and foothe my heart.

Oh! let my days like his be fpent,

In rural fhades, with mild *Content.*

3.

The Blackbird warbles on the bough,

The Milkmaid fings beneath her Cow;

The Mower, up with early dawn,

Prepares to fleece the clover'd lawn;

The Farmer views his blooming wheat *,

And ftarts the lev'ret from her feat;

* *Blooming wheat.*] The wheat's bloom is a beautiful, and very interefting, rural object; though but little, if at all, noticed by modern Poets.

Whilft

Whilſt I this lonely vale frequent,
To muſe the praiſes of *Content*.

4.

I verdant mead, and ſhady grove,
Dear ſimple ſcenes of nature, love,
And highly prize my happy lot,
That gave me one ſequeſter'd cot,
Far from the buſtles of a Crowd,
Far from the manſions of the Proud,
And gave, to crown the bleſt event,
The tranquil feelings of *Content*.

5.

Pleas'd with my little flock of ſheep,
That on my native downs I keep;
Mine are the joys of Peace and Health,
And ſure I want no greater wealth;
No vain deſires my ſoul infeſt,
Nor dwells Ambition in my breaſt.
Heav'n, all ſuch follies to prevent,
Tam'd all my thoughts to ſoft *Content*.

6. Oh!

6.

Oh ! thou from whom all comfort flows,
Whofe hand the richeft boon beftows,
Whofe careful Providence imparts,
The pureft blifs to humble hearts ;
Oh! let me never find content,
But in meek thoughts on virtue bent ;
Whilft, of thy laws enamour'd ftill,
I bow fubmiffive to thy will.

A SONG.

A S O N G.

1.

WITH Phillis alone in the grove,
  I pafs'd the ftill ev'ning away;
My fong was the tale of our love,
  She fmil'd, and approv'd of the lay.
I felt the fweet glance from her eyes,
  It open'd the way to her heart;
And Phillis could never difguife
  Her looks with the varnifh of Art.

2.

The blufh that appear'd on her face
  Out-rival'd yon rofe in the grove;
It fpoke with ineffable grace
  The wordlefs confeffion of Love;
Whilft Modefty brighten'd her charms,
  And fweet looks her affection exprefs'd,
I took the dear nymph in my arms,
  And held her with joy to my breaft.

THE

THE PARTING,

A LYRIC PASTORAL.

1.

LIFE yields no joy devoid of care,

 It is our doom awhile to part;

But whilst I go, my lovely fair,

 I leave with thee my constant heart;

Thy Colin shall, in plaintive song,

 The stories of our love rehearse;

And, as the moment glides along,

 Thy name shall fill my tender verse.

2. I'll

2.

I'll fing the well-remember'd hour,

When firft I felt thy peerlefs charms;

When firft, within this privet bow'r,

Thy beauties fill'd my circling arms;

I'll fing the fweet fequefter'd walk,

Or feat beneath yon aged thorn;

Where oft we met for tender talk,

At ev'ning mild, or dewy morn.

3.

Whilft far from Delia fadly thrown,

And by Misfortune rudely toft,

Purfu'd by Fate's malignant frown,

In all my foul's enjoyment crofs'd;

The wintry ftorms will fleet away;

I'll bear thofe ills a little while;

And keep in view that happy day,

, When thou fhalt meet me with a fmile.

4. Wilt

4.

Wilt thou, my Delia, keep thy heart

Still faithful as the turtle dove?

And let no fwain, with baleful art,

Induce thee to forget my love?

My foul to thee fhall true remain,

Till Fate, in pity to my fighs,

Relenting kindly, fhall again

Reftore thee to my longing eyes.

5.

Wilt thou frequent our fav'rite bow'r,

And wilt thou there in filence mourn,

Till time brings on the blifsful hour,

That fees thy lover's wifh'd return;

When Colin in its green alcove,

With Delia meets, no more to part;

Whilft, in that eye, the look of love,

Reftores thee to my joyful heart?

6. Whilft

6.

Whilſt on this tender theme I muſe,

    It yields my ſoul a ſoft relief;

Hope brightens up its lovely views,

    And charms away the glooms of grief:

Though Fate our envy'd bliſs delays,

    And dooms thy Colin far to rove;

Yet we ſhall end our happy days,

    United in the bands of love.

The Reader will obſerve, that the term *Lyric*

Paſtoral has been often uſed, and will, perhaps, aſk,

for what reaſon?—It is this—We often obſerve

Shepherds, and other rural characters, diverting

themſelves with ſongs, which are always, in the

proper ſenſe of the word, *ſung* to a *tune*; the verſe

of courſe muſt be *Lyric*; SHENSTONE's *Paſtoral Bal-*

lads are, for this reaſon, amongſt others, far more

natural than the Bucolics of *Theocritus*, *Virgil*, and

many more that could be named; this at leaſt is a

    I   *Welſh*

Welſh Bard's opinion, who admits of no authority but that of NATURE. We often hear the fields reſound with *Chevy Chace, Tweed Side,* and ſuch popular ſongs. *Shepherds, Ploughmen,* and *Goatherds, will often write verſes to favourite tunes* in praiſe of their *Phillidas,* their *Annies,* and their *Delias.* But we never meet with them *ſpouting* Heroics, " *ſub* " *tegmine fagi.*" At leaſt it is thus in every part of BRITAIN. But ſome, it ſeems, are of opinion that we ſhould write for other countries, climates, and times, rather than *our own.* Bravo! my good Critics!

T O

TO IVOR THE LIBERAL,

ON BEING PRESENTED BY HIM WITH A PAIR OF GLOVES.

From the Welsh of DAFYDD AP GWILYM.

IVOR THE LIBERAL, *in Welsh* IFOR HAEL, *was Lord of* BASELEG, *in the County of* MONMOUTH. *He lived about the middle of the fourteenth century, and was celebrated by the Bards of his age, and of all succeeding ages, for his unexampled liberality. He was the warm Patron of* DAFYDD AP GWILYM, *the most renowned Bard of his time, whose works are to this day held in the highest estimation.*

THIS POEM IS HUMBLY INSCRIBED TO
JOHN MORGAN, ESQ. OF TREDEGAR,
WHO EMINENTLY INHERITS THE VIRTUES OF
HIS ILLUSTRIOUS ANCESTOR.

THOU IVOR, darling of the Muse,

Who through the world thy fame pursues;

Proclaims

Proclaims thy worth in ev'ry clime,

Whilſt rapture fills her lay ſublime ;

And feels her thrilling ſoul expand,

Whilſt foſter'd by thy bounteous hand.

Thy ample gate, thy ample hall,

Are ever op'ning wide to all ;

And, warm'd in Heav'n, thy ampler mind

Dilates in Love to all mankind.

The Poor from thee with joy return,

They bleſs thy name, they ceaſe to mourn ;

And bid the Goᴅ, who knew their grief,

Reward thy hand that gave relief.

As, lately, ſitting at thy board,

Where ev'ry gueſt thy worth ador'd,

With grateful warmth I tun'd my lays,

And felt high tranſport in thy praiſe,

Whilſt noble Dukes, and Barons bold,

Sprung from thoſe Heroes fam'd of old,

United, anxious, to proclaim

The peerleſs glories of thy name ;

Name far renown'd for worth complete,

The greateſt of the truly great.

Thy favours were on all beſtow'd,

Whilſt ev'ry look with rapture glow'd ;

Thy Bard, eſteem'd the nobler gueſt,

Was with diſtinguiſh'd bounty blefs'd ;

The gifts of Nudd * could not excel

The gloves that to my portion fell ;

Surpaſſing Mordaf's * boon of old,

For both my gloves were cramm'd with gold ;

And Rhydderch's * hand could not reward

With nobler meeds his tuneful Bard.

I with thy gifts will never part,

Whilſt life's warm blood flows through my heart :

The Warrior draws his blade in vain ;

My gloves he never can obtain ;

---

* Nudd, Mordaf, and Rhydderch, are, by the Bards,
and in the *Briiſh Triadcs*, called, " The three liberal Princes of
" Britain."

Great

Great Ivor's friendſhip ſhall inſpire

His Bard with Arthur's * martial fire;

His grateful Bard, that dares advance,

Unarm'd †, againſt that warrior's lance;

* Arthur, after all the fables that have been told by
Geoffrey of *Monmouth*, and a thouſand more, was no more
than the ſon of Meiryo, the King of *Glamorgan*, elected to the
chief command of the Britiſh armies againſt the Saxons, as appears from the ancient regiſter of the cathedral chu ch of *Landaff* (ſee Carte's Hiſtory of England, vol. I. p. 202.), and
many old books of pedigrees in the Welſh language ſtill extant;
which are, to the unprejudiced, of much better authority than
the romance of Geoffrey.   One that impartially conſults
ſome genuine fragments of hiſtory, that are to be met with in
Wales, will be much inclined to think that the Ancient
Britons were never united under one hereditary Sovereign
Monarch of their own nation: the iſland of *Britain* was always
divided into a great many petty principalities, that, when occa-
ſion required, elected temporary commanders in chief to lead
their armies in caſes of invaſion; ſuch were Cassivellannus,
Cunobelinus, Caractacus, Arthur, and others.   This
opinion, however, will have no great weight with ſome Welſh-
men, who love their own nation and country better than truth.

† *Unarmed.*] It was not lawful for the Bards to bear arms;
or for any one to bear a naked weapon in their preſence. They
were deemed the *Heralds of Peace.*

And,

And, feeling Heav'n approve the deed,

Will with his blood the ravens feed.

Should my dear MORVID, kneeling, crave

What, for my fongs, lov'd IVOR gave;

Though fore to bear, I'll bid her weep,

And, fpite of Love, thy prefent keep.

Weak Vanity fhall ne'er induce,

And doom thy gloves to common ufe,

They near my heart are fafely ftor'd,

Like relics of a Saint ador'd:

Yet, fhould the Northern blaft compel,

When fnows enrobe the frozen dell,

I'll wear thy gloves, they fhall impart

Warmth to my hand, and to my heart.

Nor fhall the hand, thy bounty grac'd,

Be with a meaner glove embrac'd.

To fing thy deeds I often rove

Through ftately WENNALLT's * verdant grove,

When

---

* *Wennallt.*] One of the three manfions of IVOR, in the pa-
rifh of *Bafeleg*; *Gwern y Cleppa* was another, now in ruins; the
third,

When May difplays her floral hues,

Invites to joy the tuneful Mufe,

I feaſt with thee, thofe ſhades among,

On luxuries of ancient fong;

Strive old ANNEURIN's * heights to gain,

And emulate his lofty ſtrain.

O! let me to poetic fame

Confign thy great, thy deathlefs name,

Thy princely ſtock was ever grac'd

With martial fons, with daughters chaſte;

The nobleſt virtues all combine,

To gild the glories of thy line.

third, which has long fince difappeared, ſtood in the village of *Bafeleg.*

IVOR the LIBERAL was an anceſtor of the ancient family of MORGANS of TREDEGAR, who are defcended from MERE-DYDD GETHIN, Prince of *South Wales;* of whofe domains the TREDFOAR eftate was a very confiderable part.

* ANNEURIN.] A celebrated Bard of the fixth century, and brother to the famous GILDAS. He is called the Prince of the Britifh Bards. His *Gododin,* a noble *Heroic Poem,* is ſtill extant.

May ev'ry blessing from above,
On thee descend in dews of love !
If aught excels in bliss divine,
May that selected meed be thine ?

———————

T H E

T H E   S O N G S T E R,

A · S O N G.

1.

T H E song is my conſtant employment,

With May's plumy throng

The green woodlands among;

Thus leading the peaceable moment

Of mirth and good humour along;

When, fled from all care to my jeſſamine bow'r,

I give to the Muſe my delectable hour;

O! then 'tis my greateſt enjoyment

To breathe all my ſoul in a ſong.

2. Thus,

2.

Thus, harmony warmly careffing,

  My fancy takes wing

  Like the lark of the Spring ;

The voice of high rapture expreffing,

  I blithe with the nightingale fing :

My Phillis, the chace, or a full flowing bowl,

Are themes of my fong, the delight of my foul ;

  Sweet happinefs truly poffeffing,

  I feel myfelf great as a King.

O N

ON THE APPROACH OF WINTER,

WRITTEN IN 1778.

From the Welsh.

1.

I N woful guife the rifled groves appear,
  What dufky fogs invade the chilly dale !
Stern Winter comes in hoary mantle drear,
  With fell deftruction wings the rapid gale ;
A defpot fierce, his joylefs reign affumes,
And throngs the warring fkies with far-furrounding
    glooms.

2.

Sad Nature droops along the mournful fcene,
  Joy's glowing fmiles the fullen morn forfake ;
The hollow blaft flies ireful o'er the green,
  With furious whirl unrobes the ruftling brake ;

The

The plumy tenants of the murm'ring wood

Hide from the fcowling winds, in melancholy mood.

3.

See how the leaves are fcatter'd o'er the ground,

In hues of death beftrew the wither'd grafs !

The fea-gulls flit with doleful note around,

As vagrant o'er the ruin'd fields they pafs :

Dark fkies withhold the Sun's enfeebled ray,

And veil with fhades of Night the fable face of day.

4.

Here triumph'd once the blifsful feafon gay,

When peace, when love, wak'd up the rofy dawn.;

Whilft pipe and tabor hail'd the floral May,

Where fportive Beauty mantled o'er the lawn;

With warblers wild the vernal copfe along,

That join'd the rural Bard in foul-rejoicing fong.

5.

Now comes, from polar fkies, the gelid gale,

Or, in Atlantic ftorms, the pelting rain ;

Now

Now rolls the torrent rude along the vale,

    Its doleful murmur faddens all the plain :

Old Ocean's thronging waves indignant roar,

And burft in curling foam terrific on the fhore.

6.

Whilft mingling rigours fill the troubled air,

    On fnowy lawns recline the fodder'd flocks ;

To fhelt'ring dells the fhiv'ring doves repair,

    And fleep the fwallows in their cavern'd rocks * ;

The pallid morn that hears no cheerful found,

Wrapp'd in deep gloom appears, and Sadnefs reigns

    around.

---

* About the year 1768, the Author, with two or three more, found a great number of fwallows, in a torpid ftate, clinging in clufters to each other by their bills, in a cave of the fea cliffs, near *Dunraven Caftle,* in the county of *Glamorgan.* They revived after they had been fome hours in a warm room, but died in a day or two after, though all poffible care had been taken of them.

7.

Yet loves the Mufe to note the dreary fcene,

 Far on the wafte, or near the founding flood;

Sighs with fad echoes o'er the cheerlefs green,

 Or penfive wanders in the darkling wood;

Eyes Nature's grief with ruminating thought,

And drops the briny tear with filent anguifh fraught.

8.

So droops forlorn the melancholy mind,

 Seems like December, elad in woful plight;

With fighs congenial meets the plaintive wind,

 The mental Suns withhold their cheering light:

Life's aggregating glooms o'erwhelm the foul,

And o'er the wounded thought the waves of anguifh

 roll.

9.

Whilft, rudely torn from calm felicity,

 My days I wafte in unavailing grief;

No fortune fmiles, no pity mourns for me,

 Struck by the ftorm, I vainly feek relief;

The

The fong might foothe, or Fancy's lively ftrains,
But thefe forfake the breaft where Grief tyrannic
reigns.

10.

What, though the gentle Mufe on me beftows
Her genial favours with parental hand;
Can verfe difpel Misfortune's bitter woes?
'Th' unweary'd fpite of adverfe Fate withftand?
Oft as the charmer bids her fong refound,
Black Envy clips her wings, and chains her to the
ground.

11.

Thou, fweet Content, in robe angelic drefs'd,
Thy lenient balm can heal my wounded heart;
Come, and difpel the glooms that fill my breaft,
Thy genial fun-fhine to my foul impart;
Still the rough tempeft of my wintry day,
And bid my calmer eve unruffled pafs away.

THE POWER OF LOVE,

A   S O N G.

1.

I VIEW the world with heedlefs eye,
   Wealth, Pomp, and Pow'r, what paltry things ?
Let fuch deceitful trafh fupply
   The wants of Knaves, the pride òf Kings ;
Of Nature's nobler joys poffefs'd,
   My wifh obtain'd, my Delia's love,
The foul of tranfport fills my breaft,
I fing, and emulate the blefs'd
    That dwell in realms above.

2. Though

2.

Though doom'd with thee, my lovely fair,

O'er Libya's burning fands to ftray,

Love can refrefh the torrid air,

Thy fmile difarm the fcorching ray ;

Employ'd on thee, this joyful tongue

Shall to the wafte my paffion tell ;

I 'll walk the favage wilds along,

And, in excefs of glowing fong,

On thee, my charmer, dwell.

3.

Though banifh'd far, where polar fkies

Frown on the dreary glens below ;

Where through deep glooms the whirlwind flies,

Where Winter heaps th' eternal fnow ;

The glowing heart can there beguile

The rigours of an endlefs froft ;

Cheer up to joy the defart ifle,

And warm, with Love's refulgent fmile,

The long-benighted coaft.

4. The

4.

The thunder's peal, the madden'd ftorm,

   The furge that fwells with Alpine height,

Fell Danger, in each haggard form,

   Can ne'er my dauntlefs heart affright;

Amid Misfortune's rude excefs,

   Whilft Horror makes all nature quake;

Cheer'd by thy looks in all diftrefs,

I 'll tune the fong of Happinefs,

   And fuffer for thy fake.

DAVONA'S

D A V O N A'S   V A L E.

WRITTEN IN 1777,

On arriving in the COUNTRY, *after a Refidence of fome Years in* LONDON.

1.

NO more of LONDON's hateful noife!

 Ye madden'd crowds adieu;

Detefting *Art's* ungenial joys,

 I dwell no more with you:

Hail, dear GLAMORGAN, let me greet

 Once more the favour'd plain;

I fly with gladden'd foul to meet

 My native cot again.

2. Ye

2.

Ye dappled fields, ye lawns belov'd,

 Where erſt, in tuneful mood,

I tun'd my pipe, with Fancy rov'd,

 The rural Muſe purſu'd;

Your lovely ſcenes again I view,

 Your healthful breeze inhale;

Youth's early ſchemes of bliſs renew,

 In lone *Davona's Vale.*

3.

Delicious Vale! by Nature dreſs'd

 In Beauty's rich array;

Here let me waſte, in mental reſt,

 My peaceful days away:

And let my ſoul on virtue bent,

 Attend bright Wiſdom's tale;

She, with that Angel, call'd Content,

 Dwell's in *Davona's Vale.*

4. Here

4.

Here Memory recalls again
  What, lisping, erst I sung;
When first the Muse, in simple strain,
  Inform'd my fault'ring tongue.
I 'll seek her in the wonted bow'r,
  Beneath yon aged thorn;
Where oft I spent the blissful hour
  In Youth's romantic morn.

5.

Youth still in calmer mood remains,
  Still doth its warmth impart;
Though Grief has planted all her pains,
  Deep in this injur'd heart.
Here, where no guileful arts beset,
  I lull my soul to peace;
Forgive my foes, my wrongs forget,
  And bid resentment cease.

6. Lon-

6.

LONDON, thou den of hell-born Art,
   I bid thy filth adieu;
Why did I truſt my ſimple heart
   With thy deceitful crew ?
With eager flight, with anxious mind,
   I ſeek my native ſhore;
And leave thy tinſel glare behind,
   And dream of thee no more.

7.

Far from thy venom'd ſkies I dwell,
   In rural cot unknown;
Where Peace and Health enrich my cell,
   Their treaſures are my own:
My ſoul ſhall execrate the day,
   When Folly told her tale;
Beguil'd my heart, and bid me ſtray
   From fair *Davona's Vale.*

4

8. Re-

8.

Returning to maternal plains,

   I tune my joyful song ;

Bid Echo chaunt my sylvan strains,

   Their winding dales along.

Lov'd objects meet my partial eyes,

   Familiar paths I trace ;

And hail once more these happy skies,

   And bless my native place.

9.

From wonted labours of the day,

   When fall the dews around,

In thoughtful mood, I bend my way,

   Far o'er the trackless ground;

Whilst, from her solitary brake,

   The love-lorn Nightingale

Keeps the sweet plaintive Muse awake

   In still *Davona's Vale.*

10. Here,

10.

Here, in the calm of Solitude,

I Nature's lore purfue ;

Mad Mirth, I bid thy clamours rude,

Thy giggling tribe adieu.

Love nurtur'd Senfibility

Shall occupy my heart ;

Sweet warmth of Heav'n ! what blifs to me

Thy tender thrills impart !

11.

My fober Mufe difdains to flit

Around the midnight bowl ;

No frantic lays of fpurious wit

Can pleafe my penfive foul :

The plaintive fong yields more delight,

Soft Pity's tender wail,

As, devious, in the dufk of night,

I range *Davona's Vale.*

12. When

12.

When Larks proclaim the dewy dawn,
  And Blackbirds mount the spray,
I walk the grove, or flow'ry lawn,
  As Fancy points the way;
The varied landscape glads my sight,
  I breathe its balmy gale;
And taste of Nature's true delight
  In calm *Davona's Vale.*

13.

Here, charm'd with Beauty's varied hues,
  I pass the vernal morn;
Where charms that captivate the Muse
  The bloomy scenes adorn.
Come, tuneful guest, O! come along,
  With sweet entrancing tale;
Rapt echoes shall repeat thy song,
  Wide o'er *Davona's Vale.*

14. Thou,

14.

Thou, tenant meek of humble plains,

Heart-folacing Content ;

I join thy band of rural fwains,

Thy tranquil fhades frequent.

O ! let me, far from care and ftrife,

At thy rich board regale ;

And fpend what yet remains of life

In dear *Davona's* * *Vale*.

* *Davona.*] Welfh, *Dawon* ; Englifh, *Daw*. A river of *Glamorgan*, that, running through the town of *Cowbridge*, and by the village of *Flimfton*, the Author's place of abode, falls into the *Severn* fea at, and forms the harbour of, *Aberthaw*, or *Aberdduwon*.

END OF THE FIRST VOLUME.

www.ingramcontent.com/pod-product-compliance
Lightning Source LLC
Chambersburg PA
CBHW030758020726
47499CB00006B/1680